By Stephen Gould

Jumper
Jumper: Griffin's Story

JUMPER:
GRIFFIN'S STORY

Steven Gould is the author of *Jumper*, *Wildside*, *Helm*, *Blind Waves*, *Reflex*, and *Jumper: Griffin's Story*, as well as several short stories. He is the recipient of the Hal Clement Young Adult Award for Science Fiction and has been on the Hugo ballot twice and the Nebula ballot once for his short fiction. Steve lives in New Mexico with his wife, writer Laura J. Mixon and their two daughters. As he is somewhere between Birth and Death, he considers himself to be middle-aged.

Steven Gould

JUMPER:
GRIFFIN'S STORY

HARPER
Voyager

Harper*Voyager*
An imprint of HarperCollins*Publishers*
77–85 Fulham Palace Road,
Hammersmith, London W6 8JB

First published in Great Britain by HarperCollins*Publishers* 2008

This paperback edition 2008
1

A catalogue record for this book is
available from the British Library

ISBN-13: 978 0 00 727600 4

Set in Times

Printed in Great Britain by Clays Ltd, St Ives plc

Mixed Sources

Product group from well-managed
forests and other controlled sources
www.fsc.org   Cert no. SW-COC-1806
© 1996 Forest Stewardship Council

FSC

FSC is a non-profit international organisation established
to promote the responsible management of the world's forests.
Products carrying the FSC label are independently certified
to assure consumers that they come from forests that are managed
to meet the social, economic and ecological needs
of present and future generations.

Find out more about HarperCollins and the environment at
www.harpercollins.co.uk/green

For Ralph Vicinanza—Life Changer

A Note About This Novel

My previous novels featuring teleportation, *Jumper* and *Reflex,* are the basis for the upcoming New Regency/Fox movie *Jumper,* to be released in early 2008. Like most novel-to-movie projects, the story's events and circumstances mutate through the process of adaptation. *This* novel was written to be consistent with the movie, and, as a consequence, there are significant differences between its world and the world of the previous novels.

JUMPER:
GRIFFIN'S STORY

ONE

The Empty Quarter

Every couple of months Dad and I would climb in the car and he'd drive out through the suburbs, out past the small towns, past the farms and ranches, until we came to what I called the Empty Quarter. I saw a BBC special on it once—I thought they said Ruby Kallie, but now I know they were saying the Rub al-Khali—the "quarter of emptiness."

It's the sea of sand that makes up a fifth of the Arabian Peninsula, but for us it could mean Death Valley, or the Gila wilderness, or the Spanish Pyrenees, and once, it was an island in the Bay of Siam that we had to sail a small boat to.

But it had to be empty—it had to be without people. That was the only safe place where I could do it, where I could practice.

"We just can't chance it, Griff. You want to do this, this is the only way."

We were living in the United States then, five thousand miles from England, in San Diego, in a garage flat at the north end of Balboa Park, but when Dad said that, we were a hundred miles east of the flat. We'd taken the Yuma cutoff, U.S. 98 off of Interstate 8, and it was hot and windy and sand was blowing across the road.

I was only nine then, used to not knowing anything, always asking, always pushing. "Then why do it at all—why should we even take this chance?"

He looked sideways at me and sighed, then back to the road, swerving slightly to avoid a bouncing tumbleweed the size of a Volkswagen. "It comes down to . . . could you do that? Could you walk away from it? I mean, for me, it would be like spending the rest of my life in a wheelchair, even though I could still walk. I'd be pretending I could do naught, you know, making myself do everything the hard way when by just standing up and taking a few steps I could reach that stuff off the wheelchair ramp, the stuff on the upper shelf."

He sped up a little as we reached a rocky stretch where

there wasn't quite so much blowing sand. "And, dammit, it's a gift! Why the hell shouldn't you be able to do it? Just because they—" He clamped his mouth shut and looked back at the road.

For once I didn't push it. There were some things my parents just wouldn't talk about, and what happened back in Oxford was one of them. When I'd first jumped, at five, from the steps of the Martyr's Memorial in front of a busload of tourists. Well, not then, exactly, but after, the thing that caused us to leave the UK and keep moving.

Dad began watching the odometer closely, checking the map. He hadn't been there before—our Empty Quarters were always different. He drove past the road, only recognizing the turn after we passed because a tangle of tumbleweeds hid the cattle guard that marked it. We were the only ones on the highway—he just backed up and made the turn, switching the Range Rover into four-wheel as soon as he was in the loose sand on the other side of the grate.

"Tell me the rules," he said.

"Go on, Dad!" I knew the rules. I'd known them since I was six.

"So, back to the flat? It's two hours, but I'll do it."

I held up my hand. "All right, all right!" I held up four fingers and ticked them off one by one. "Never jump where someone can see me. Never jump near home. Never jump to or from the same place twice. And never, never, *ever* jump unless I must—or unless you or Mum tell me to."

"And what does that mean—that you *must*?"

"If I'm going to get hurt or captured."

"Killed or captured by who?"

"Anyone." *Them.* That's all I knew. The strangers from Oxford.

"And what does it mean if you break the rules?"

"Have to move. Again."

"Yeah. Again."

We drove for another forty-five minutes, though it was slow going. "This'll have to do. Any farther and we'll be too close to the border. Don't want to attract the INS." He turned up a dry wash and went on until we couldn't see the road and the hills of the ravine rose up on both sides.

It took us ten minutes to climb to the top of the higher ridge, so we could see all around. Dad used his binoculars, taking *forever.* Finally he said, "Okay. In the ravine only, right-oh?"

I danced in place. *"Now?"*

He said, "Now."

I looked down at the Rover, toy-sized, at the bottom of the ravine, and then I was there, sand settling around me as I fumbled with the gate.

By the time Dad had hiked back down I'd changed into the coveralls and the goggles and I had the face mask hanging loosely around my neck. When he came trudging across the sand and gravel, I was laying out the paintball gun and the hopper full of rounds and the CO_2 cartridges.

He took a drink from the water bottle and offered it to me. While I drank he put on his own goggles and loaded the gun.

"Don't wait for me to fire. This is pretty fast—maybe two hundred feet per second—but you could still jump before it arrived if you were far enough away. But bullets travel thousands of feet per second. You wait till they fire, and you'll be dead.

"Don't let anyone even *point* a weapon at you."

I was just seating the face mask when he shot me, point-blank, in the thigh.

"Fuck!" I yelled, grabbing my leg. The paint was red and I put one of my hands right in it.

"What did you say?" Dad looked half mad, half amused. I could swear he was trying not to laugh.

I blinked, looking down at the red paint on my hand. My leg hurt. It hurt a lot, but I wasn't supposed to use that word. I opened my mouth to reply but Dad said, "Never mind," and lifted the gun again.

Fool me once, shame on you. Fool me twice . . .

The paintball splattered across the gravel, but I was twenty feet off to the side. Dad twisted and got off a quick shot but the reason it didn't hit me was that he missed, not that I'd jumped in time. I felt the wind of the projectile go past my head but then I was on the far side of the truck and the second shot passed through empty air, before tumbling through the branches of a creosote bush.

"Okay," he yelled. "Hide-and-seek, unlimited."

I turned around and began counting loudly. I heard his feet crunch across gravel and then nothing. The second I counted thirty, I jumped sideways, thirty feet, expecting to hear the *poooof* of the paintball gun, but Dad was nowhere in sight.

There were several stretches of sand in the wash and one of these had a fresh set of widely spaced tracks leading across it. I jumped to the stretch of sand without crossing the gravel and followed them.

I had to find him without getting shot. But I could jump as much as I wanted. Around a bend in the ravine, the tracks were closer together but they went another fifty feet and stopped in the middle of the wash. Stopped.

Dad wasn't there, either, and there wasn't anything nearby he could have stepped onto. For just a second, I thought, Maybe . . . maybe Dad could—

The paintball caught me on the butt. It didn't hurt near as much as the last one but it hurt my pride. I spun and jumped at the same time, sideways, ten feet, sloppy—there must've been ten pounds of dirt falling away from me and jump rot hanging in the air where I'd been. Twisting, fading jump rot.

Dad was stepping out from behind some scrub. The gun hung loosely at his side.

I pointed at the line of tracks in the sand. "Did you jump?"

He laughed, almost a bark. "Don't I wish! I just turned around and walked back in my tracks." He pointed at some rocks near his hiding place. "Stepped off the sand there and Bob's your uncle." He pointed his finger at the ground and twirled it like he was stirring a drink. "Again."

I turned around and started counting loudly. As he ran off he shouted over his shoulder, "Look for more than tracks in the sand!"

And that's the sort of thing we did for the next hour. We did hide-and-seek, limited (where I couldn't jump until I saw him), and tag, where I had to jump close enough to touch him and get away without getting shot, and closed room, where we drew a big square in the sand and I could jump anywhere in it but not leave it, while he fired shot after shot.

Once he hit a patch of jump rot where I'd been and the paintball exploded, coming back out as high-velocity pieces of plastic film and a mist of spray paint. Another time, I jumped late and the paintball came with me, tumbling through the brush at right angles to its original path, but missing me.

Dad was perplexed. "Wow, I don't think I've ever seen it do that before." Dad had this theory that the jump rot was like, well, like the wake of a ship, the disruption of the water when a vessel passes through. It's like the turbulence or maybe even a hole I leave behind.

When I jump in a hurry, sloppily, there's more of it and I carry more crap with me. When I'm focused, if there *is* jump rot, it's tiny, and fades away almost instantly.

We continued. When Dad said, "Enough," I had one more paint mark on my right shoulder blade, but he'd gone through seventy paintball rounds. He let me shoot a dozen rounds at a boulder, enough to finish off the last of the CO_2 cartridge, and then we went home.

He never said anything about my swearing and I never said anything about him shooting me in the leg.

Call it even.

Tuesday and Thursday afternoons I had karate class.

Mum had a doctorate in French literature but she didn't work. She was homeschooling me. She said that I just got too bored in the public education system, but I heard them talking once, when they thought I was asleep.

Dad said, "What can we do about it? He's too young to hold a secret this big all the time. It's not fair to him and it's too dangerous. Maybe later, when he's older."

Mum said, "He's not a kid. No kid ever talked like that— he's a miniature adult. He needs to run up against kid logic and skin his knees where we're not there to pick him up. He needs to make friends."

The compromise was karate class. The homeschooling curriculum required a physical education equivalent so I had to do something.

I think Dad went for it because of the discipline and because he thought, from the class he watched, that the kids never talked to each other. Well, we weren't supposed to talk *during* class but it was an after-school program at the elementary school two blocks away—all form-one kids. Of course there was talking.

I liked our instructor, Sensei Torres. He didn't play favorites and he was very gentle and he was very careful to keep Paully MacLand in check.

Paully was in fifth grade for the second time and he was almost as tall as Sensei Torres. He'd been doing the karate program since first grade and had a green belt.

And he was mean.

We were doing two-step *kumite* partner practice. One person would attack with a punch and the other would block and counterpunch. I was working with Paully and he wasn't interested in the exercise. He was interested in hurting.

There was a definite no-contact rule. If you kicked or punched you had to stop short of hitting anybody. It was a firm rule and anyone who broke it had to sit out and *could* get dropped from the class if he kept doing it. Paully knew that. One of the kids told me Paully was kicked out of the class back in fourth grade for repeated offenses and was only allowed back the next year.

What Paully did instead was turn his blocks into strikes. He'd block so hard, it hurt—it left bruises. Like, perhaps, a paintball round in the thigh, point-blank.

I didn't swear this time, though. I gritted my teeth instead and kept going. To hit so hard, Paully was drawing back, cocking before the block, which required he start almost before I actually punched. Next time it was my turn, I broke my rhythm, stepping in, but delaying the punch slightly. He blocked and missed my arm entirely. My punch stopped just short of his nose.

Sensei Torres laughed and had everybody change partners. Later he said to me privately, "Good eyes, Griff. It was

21

bad karate. In a real fight, you can't block a strike that hasn't even started."

But Paully was waiting when I finished changing for the walk home, just inside the locker room, blocking the door. "So, you limey ass-licker, think you're somethin' with that stutter punch? Think you can make me look bad in front of Sensei?"

Maybe Dad was right about me having trouble keeping my mouth shut. It just came out, unbidden.

"Bollocks. You don't need *me* to look bad. You do that all by yourself." Right away I was sorry I said it, scared, in fact, but how do you take something like that back, especially when you mean it?

He just charged, rage painted on his face like red paint, his fist cocked back and looking larger than any paintball.

I couldn't help it. Really, I didn't mean to do it, I didn't mean to break the rule, but one second his fist was heading toward my face like a thrown rock and the next I was standing in a cloud of dust in a ravine, next to a paintball-splattered boulder, out in the Empty Quarter.

I'd just broken rules number one and two (don't jump near home and don't jump where someone can see me) and maybe even rule four (don't jump unless I must—if I'm going to get killed or captured).

I was in *so* much trouble.

So I lied.

I jumped back to the school, outside, in the hollow between

the stairs and a hedge where I sometimes waited before karate, before the last bell rang. I used to sit in there and watch, invisible, the outsider—the foreign homeschooler—and watch all the kids run off, met by their parents or playing with each other on the playground.

I waited until I saw Paully leave, walking odd, looking back at the school with wide eyes. I exhaled. He looked okay. My worry was that he'd run into the jump rot before it faded.

It only takes five minutes to walk home. I did it in two.

"How was class?" Mum asked when I pounded up the steps and into the kitchen. She glanced at the clock. "Did you run?"

"Uh, yeah. Thirsty." I buried my face in the fridge. I could feel my ears burning. I *never* lied to Mum. Well, technically it wasn't lying but they'd always been clear about lying by omission.

I came out with the Gatorade. Mum had already pulled a glass from the dishwasher. She gave me a quick squeeze around the shoulders then set the glass on the counter. "Pork pie for supper. Potatoes or rice?"

"Rice."

"Broccoli or green beans?"

I made a face. "Broccoli, if we have to."

She laughed. "Well, there's pudding after."

I nodded and headed for my room, but she snagged me by the collar. "Are you all right?" She put the back of her hand against my forehead.

"What?"

"You didn't ask what kind of pudding. I'm thinkin' some terminal illness, maybe Ebola."

"Ha-ha. Okay, what kind?"

"Raspberry tart."

I said, "Brilliant!" to please her, but the truth was the thought of food made my stomach clench into a hard little knot. "I think I'll just go and try another unit of math, okay?"

She took an exaggerated step back from me. "Or it could be bubonic plague. But go—mine is not to question why. This may not last—it could be a fluke, a temporary aberration. Let's not mess with it."

As I walked back to my room I heard her saying, "And maybe he'll do a science unit and a history unit and maybe a French essay or two. If only we could find this germ, the I'll-go-do-schoolwork germ, we could market it. Mothers everywhere would worship at my feet. Dare I say sainthood? It could hap—"

I shut my bedroom door loudly.

Paully would probably never say anything. I mean, what could he say? He was the kind of boy who didn't like looking stupid, probably because he *was* stupid. Would he be stupid enough to tell this story? If he just said I scampered like a baby that would be fine. I wouldn't care about that.

I did a unit of long division since I said I would. Actually, I rather liked math. Everything works or it doesn't. There isn't anything gray about it. And every time I stopped working on the math problems, I started thinking about Paully and my jumping. Even drawing, my usual escape, didn't work.

I did *three* units of math.

Mum and Dad were talking about an upcoming business trip at dinner so I didn't have to say much. I knew if I didn't eat, they'd really begin to suspect something. I ate as much as I could but it sat in my stomach like lead.

"What are you thinking about, Griff?"

"What? Uh, nothing, Dad."

"You've been staring at the wall for five minutes. No moving fingers, I hope? *Mene mene tekel upharsin* and all that."

Dad's a bit odd sometimes. "Math, I guess. And I was thinking about karate today. And when we did paintball out in the desert." All true. All lies.

He nodded. Both of them watched me and it felt like the truth was written across my forehead. I could feel my ears heating up. "I don't understand why things repeat sometimes to infinity."

It was my best distraction. When in doubt, always ask a math question or a question about *Le Petit Prince*. Either could occupy them for hours, avoiding whatever they'd been on about. The downside was, well, it could occupy them for hours.

"What do you mean?"

"Like ten divided by three. You know—the answer is three point three three three three three three three and so on. Forever, I guess. But does it go on forever? How do they know? Maybe after enough times it becomes two? Or four? They call it a rational number, but really—what's rational about *that*?"

25

So Mum pulled down a pad of paper and Dad pulled out an old textbook and by the time I escaped to my room, an hour and a half later, they were showing each other that it was really a function of a base-ten numbering system. "Yeah, if you divide ten by three in base nine, you get three."

I shut the door to my room and flopped facedown onto my bed. I should have told them. I wanted to tell them. But I didn't want to move *again*.

I changed for bed early, and tried to lose myself in reading, in drawing, even math. Later I brushed my teeth without being asked, causing more comments from Mum. She came in and kissed me good night. Dad stood in the doorway, said, "Good dreams, Griff."

Mum asked, "You want the door shut?"

"Yeah."

"Bonne nuit, mon cher."

Normally I'm asleep in minutes but this time I couldn't get it out of my head. I'd lied about *it*. I'd broken the rules.

So they'll never know. Only Paully saw and who would believe him, even if he talked?

I buried my head under my pillow but it didn't help. *I'd* know. Didn't matter if Mum and Dad found out. I'd always know.

I got up. I could hear them—well, I could hear the TV. They always watched the late news together and drank a cup of herbal tea. It was part of their routine, their last thing before bedtime. Sometimes I'd sneak down the hall and watch from the corner. Half the time Mum would doze off during the sports and Dad would tease her about it.

I eased open my door. I had to tell them. Whatever happened, I had to tell them. I took a step out into the hall and the doorbell rang.

I felt a jolt in the stomach. *Paully? His parents? Someone from the school?*

Dad turned off the TV before he went to the door, followed by Mum, yawning. She hadn't fallen asleep yet—the news was on the weather. She saw me in the doorway and blinked, started to frown.

I heard Dad open the door—it was around the corner past the kitchen so I couldn't see it from the hall.

"Mr. O'Conner?" It was a woman's voice. "I'm so sorry to drop by this late, but I'd like to talk to you about Griffin. I'm from the Homeschooling Administration Department at SDSD."

Mum's head snapped around. "No, you're not."

"Beg your pardon?" the woman's voice said.

"You're not. It's not the SDSD. It's the San Diego *Unified* School District or the San Diego *City Schools*. And there is no department for homeschooling. It's done through the charter schools."

"Fine. Have it your way," said the woman. Her voice, previously warm and apologetic, went hard like granite.

Mum took a step away from the door and I saw her eyes get really big. Her hand down at her side jerked toward me and pointed back, a clear indication to go back into my room.

I took a step back but I left the door open so that I could still hear, but what I heard was Dad saying, "Put the knife down. We're not armed. What do you want?"

There was a crash from my parents' room, at the other end of the hall.

Back at the door a man's voice, a Brit from Bristol by the accent, said, "Where's your kiddle?"

Dad shouted, "Griff—" There was a thud and his voice cut off. Mum screamed and I jumped—

—into the living room, magazine pages flying through the air, books falling off the bookshelf.

Dad was on his knees, one hand to his head. There were two strange men and the woman in the living room and they all twisted as I appeared, much faster than Dad ever managed, odd-shaped guns coming to bear. I flinched away, into the kitchen, plates and cups shattering against the wall and sink, and heard the guns fire, muffled, not unlike the paint gun, but there was an odd whipping noise, and they were turning again, right to me by the refrigerator. Mum screamed "Go!" and shoved one of the men into the other but the woman still fired and it burned my neck and I was standing by the boulder, the moonlit, paint-splattered boulder two hundred miles away.

I jumped back, but not to the kitchen. I appeared in the dark garage below and scrambled up onto the workbench, to reach the shelf above, where Dad kept the paint gun. Steps pounded down the outside stairs and then someone kicked the door, to force it open, but there was a drop bar—it was that kind of neighborhood.

I put a CO_2 cartridge in the gun. The top of the door splintered but held. I fumbled a tubular magazine of paintballs into the gun as a chunk of door fell into the room. The fat barrel of one of the weird guns appeared in the gap and I jumped, this time to my room.

Steps pounded down the hall and I jumped again, back to the living room. A man held a knife to Mum's throat and Dad lay on the ground, still.

I shot the man in the eyes, point-blank.

He screamed and fell backward, clawing at his eyes. A gun went off and something tore at my hip and I jumped sideways again, shooting the man who was coming up the hallway in the forehead. One hand went to his face but he fired his weapon and multiple projectiles with wires between them tore through the air over my head. I jumped behind him and he whirled and I shot him in the bollocks, twice.

He doubled over and as he did, I saw Mum.

She was lying on the floor, slumped to one side, and the blood was everywhere.

Plaster exploded next to my head as a trio of projectiles thudded into the wall, wire trailing, lashing at the paint. I dropped to my knees, half flinching, half numb.

Dad's puddle of blood was even bigger and there was a knife sticking out of his lower back.

The man I'd shot in the bollocks was twisting around,

bringing his gun up. I shot him in the face again, hitting his cheekbone. He fired his gun but the cables flew down the hallway, over my head, tearing pictures off both walls. I hit him with the paintball gun barrel, hit him hard, and again, and again. He dropped his gun and his eyes rolled back.

I turned back to Mum and Dad and the door. I could hear footsteps on the stair. I lifted the paintball gun but there was a flash from the door and a projectile caught the gun, slammed it up into my forehead.

I fell back, my vision dimming, dropping into some dark and formless place, but instead of hitting the wall, I fell all the way back onto sand and gravel.

The Empty Quarter. *Mum. Dad.* Empty.

I tried to lift my head and the moon dimmed and blinked out.

Empty.

TWO

Lost (and Found)

Someone was trickling water into my mouth and, startled, I inhaled it. Wracking coughs produced a stabbing pain in my head and side, but I couldn't stop. The sun was high and blinding. I squeezed my eyes shut, still coughing. There was something wrong with my forehead and the side of my neck and my right hip.

Hands lifted me, helping me to sit. I managed a wheezing breath without coughing and opened my eyes. Sand. Gravel.

The Empty Quarter. I touched my forehead—there was a ragged gash, crusted, above my right eyebrow. I dropped farther and felt the side of my neck. There was a scab, like a rug burn. It tugged when I turned my head to see who was helping me to sit up.

"*¿Mas comodo?*" a rough voice asked. White teeth flashed in a salt-and-pepper beard. I shifted back slightly. He wore a straw hat and a blinding white button-down shirt, worn khaki shorts. His eyes were hidden behind mirrored aviator shades. His skin was brown but he didn't look Hispanic. Tanned.

"Excuse me?" I managed.

"Oh," he said. "More water?" He offered me the plastic bottle.

I accepted it and sipped cautiously, trying not to breathe it again.

"What happened, kid?"

I blinked. What *had* happened? Something at home, the woman who said she was from the school district . . . ?

I think I screamed then. I know I jerked upright and surged to my feet and my vision dimmed.

Not sure how much time passed, but I was lying down again, on my back. Someone was holding something over me, which shaded my face from the sun. It was a black umbrella and I could see the sun shining through the black cloth and the spokes, spotted with rust. The hand holding it was thin and wrinkled. I followed the arm to a woman with jet black hair, wrinkled brown skin, and dark eyes like still pools of night.

She saw me watching her and said something in Spanish, to the side. I started to sit up again and a hand, not hers, pressed me back down.

"Let's not and say we did." It was the bearded man from before. "Unless you want to pass out again. There's a nice puddle of dried blood here. Didn't see it before—you were lying on it, but I'd say you're better off lying down, okay?"

The wracking sobs came then. I remembered it all, every bit, flashing over and over, from Mum screaming "Go!" to the blood and the motionless eyes staring into nothing.

I think I passed out again.

The light was different—the sun had shifted halfway across the sky and the wind had picked up. Instead of an umbrella, a blue plastic tarp shaded my entire body, flapping gently in the slight breeze. A clear plastic bag half filled with fluid twisted and bounced with the movement of the tarp. A tube dropped from the bag and I watched it for several minutes before realizing it was running into my arm.

Crunching footsteps crossing the gravel came closer and then the light changed again as someone stuck his head into the shelter.

"*¿Estas despierto?*" It was the woman from before, the one with the umbrella. She watched my face for some sign of comprehension, then tried, "You okay?"

"Okay? Yes, uh, *si. No hablo español.*"

"Okay. Good. Okay." She pointed to a plastic bottle lying beside me, mostly full of water. She mimed tilting a bottle up to her mouth. "Okay?"

"Right. Uh, okay."

I tried to sit up but she shook her head. "No. Descanza. Estate quietecito."

I dropped back. My head spun from the slight effort to sit up. I explored my side and found a mass of gauze and tape on my hip. I found a smaller bandage on my forehead, running up into my hair, the tape tugging painfully when I touched it. I wasn't on the ground, I realized, but lying on a stretcher, one of those canvas things with two poles locked apart. Turning my head without lifting it, I realized we were no longer in my gully but on some raised hillside. I could see miles across desert, over gullies and low hills.

They'd moved me.

Driven me? Carried me?

I thought about the night before and it was as if I were stuck, frozen. My mind just stopped working. I didn't pass out but I lay there staring at the ceiling trying to think but it was too much—my mind was just shying away from it. I *knew* it had happened. It was the gauze on my head. My brain was wrapped in gauze—white, fuzzy gauze—and it was hard to feel stuff through it.

I heard someone shout from far away, "Hey, Consuelo! *¡Un poco ayuda!*" The woman sitting beside me patted me again on the shoulder and ducked out under the edge of the tarp.

As soon as she was standing upright I heard her footsteps go from a walk to a jogging run. After a minute footsteps returned, more than two, but there was a dragging sound, too, and then the bearded man and Consuelo were back, a man supported between them. His face was bloody and swollen and though his limbs twitched as if to help support him, he was helpless as a baby.

The bearded man glanced at me, watching, and said, "Hey, pardner, think you can get out of that stretcher? Got someone here who needs it worse."

I blinked, then sat up carefully. The bandages at my hip tugged and my head swam just a bit but my vision didn't dim like it had before. I edged off the stretcher away from the newcomer, then slid the stretcher toward them, holding it steady as they put the newcomer down.

There was a rapid exchange in Spanish of which the only word I understood was "banditos" and they were working as they talked. Consuelo was wiping blood off the man's face as the bearded man hung another bag of liquid from the same line that supported mine. He cleaned a spot on the inside of the man's elbow with a wipe from a tear-open packet and then slid a needle into the skin.

I winced and looked away. When I turned back, the needle was connected to the tube hanging down from the bag. The wind died for a moment, then shifted around, and I could smell him. He smelled awful, like one of the dirtier homeless guys around Balboa Park—rancid sweat and a whiff of urine.

"Uh, need a loo . . . bathroom." My voice was a rasping croak but understandable.

The bearded guy was putting a foam collar around the neck of the man on the stretcher. He looked up at me. "Really? That's a good sign." He reached over and pinched the back of my hand.

I jerked it away. "Hey!"

He shook his head, chuckling. "Pinch the skin on the back of your hand and let go. Where I can see."

"Why?"

"Dehydration. The longer the skin stays tented, the more dehydrated you are."

"Oh." I held my hand up, palm down, and did what he asked. The skin pulled back flat pretty much as soon as I let go.

"Hold still," he said. I froze and he peeled back the strip of tape securing my drip needle, then pulled it out, one quick, smooth movement. I felt a tug and then there was a red dot welling up. He handed me an antiseptic wipe. "Put pressure on it with that—hold it high. While you're peeing you can close your elbow over it." He put his own finger over the inside of his elbow and pinned it by folding his arm up.

"Where's the loo—uh, toilet?"

He laughed. "Pick a rock."

I ducked gingerly out from under the tarp. My head spun and I bent over for a moment, bracing my hands on my thighs. After another moment things settled and I straightened carefully.

There was a battered four-wheel-drive pickup parked between two boulders, so dusty I couldn't tell what color the paint job was. A large pair of binoculars and a battered orange-and-white ice chest sat on the tailgate. Two camp chairs sat in the partial shade of a mesquite bush.

The pressure in my bladder reminded me why I was standing. I took limping steps in the direction of the largest rock down the hill and peed behind it.

It took me longer to walk up the hill than down. It wasn't just gravity. Without the full bladder I didn't have the motivation, the need, and the gravel hurt my bare feet. It was hard not to just lie down on the ground right where I was and curl up in a ball.

The bearded man ducked out of the tarp and glanced at me. "You okay?"

No! I thought, but I nodded and resumed my painful limp up the hill.

He motioned toward the camp chair. "I'm Sam," he said. "You got a name?"

"Grif—" I stopped myself. Then continued. "John Grifford. They call me Griff." The woman claiming to be from the school district had asked for *me,* for Griffin O'Conner. "What happened to him?" I gestured at the blue tarp.

"Bandits. He's a Mexican making the crossing to find work. Pretty poor but with a little money, usually everything his extended family can scratch together in U.S. dollars so he can travel to a city with jobs once he's across. There's them on both sides of the border that prey on 'em.

And after it happens, they don't think they can complain to the police on this side, and on the other side, half the time it is the police." Sam paused as I painfully lowered myself into the chair. "Now, once I heard you talk, I knew you weren't Mexican, but his story could be yours—who attacked you?"

I looked away and put my hand to my mouth. The cotton gauze threatened to shred.

He added the unbearable bit: "Where are your parents?"

I nearly jumped. It was like a blow. I knew I wasn't in danger but I still wanted to flinch away. I wanted to flee, to run, but I knew that no matter how far I went it wouldn't change the facts.

"They're d . . . d . . . DEAD!" There. I'd said it. Said something I couldn't even think.

"Where?" Sam's eyes widened a bit and his eyes twitched sideways. *"When?"*

He thinks it happened where they found me, that the people who attacked me could still be around. "San Diego—last night."

Oh, bugger. What was the point of giving him a false name? Now he'd be able to read the newspapers and figure out who I really was.

Something my dad used to say went through my head: *Better to keep your mouth shut and be thought an idiot than to speak and confirm it.*

Sam dropped his shoulders back down. "How'd you get

all the way out here? Did they dump you? Could they still be around?"

I shook my head. "I got away—I came here because it was . . . safe." I looked at the blue tarp. "Well, I thought it was safe."

"How?"

I shook my head. "Can't tell you. But honest, those that kill—" I bit down on my lip and squeezed my eyes shut for a second. "The last I saw of them was in San Diego. Not here."

He stared at me for a moment. "Well, Pablo, in there, needs some pretty urgent medical attention. We'll be putting him in the truck and then I'll radio the county EMS, meet them out at the highway. The police and the border patrol will get involved pretty quick, so I just have one question. Should we be mentioning you? I mean, you didn't go to the police in San Diego, did you?"

I stared at him. "What kind of adult are you? Of course you're going to tell the police, no matter what I say. I'm just a kid. Doesn't matter what *I* want. I'm a minor."

He blinked, then laughed without making any noise, like I'd said something funny.

"So why are you even asking?" Too strident. I clamped my mouth shut, determined not to say anything else.

He stared at me, his brow wrinkled. "Kid, something really bad happened to you and yours but all I really know is that you're in trouble. I meet people in trouble all the time. They're undocumented workers, crossing. I'm not here to judge them, either. What Consuelo and I do is try and keep them from dying. Sometimes it's just a little water, sometimes it's major medical evac. But we don't judge and we don't involve the INS unless we have to.

"I don't know what's best for you. I don't know enough about what happened or why. You're not dying—I don't have to involve the county and the police. Don't know if the cops would just take you back someplace where the people who did this could get at you again or if they even would want to get at you. So, I'm askin' and I mean it: *Should* I tell the police about you?"

I shook my head side to side, hard, and the scab on my neck tore and stung.

"Well okay, then. I won't." Sam started to get up.

Despite my best intentions, I said, "Why do you do this, helping the illegals, I mean?"

"Someone's gotta. I've been doing it for six years, since I found three dead men on the edge of my property. Consuelo, she lost her husband and teenage son east of here. Their coyote got them halfway across the worst of it and demanded more money before letting them into the truck, still out in the middle of nowhere. She got the story from a woman who didn't have to walk—who didn't die in the basin."

I licked my lips. "She had the cash?"

"She offered a *different* form of payment."

I looked at him, puzzled.

Sam said, "God, you're young. You talk like you're older so I keep forgetting. She offered sex for passage."

I felt my ears get hot.

"How old are you, kid? Eleven, twelve?"

"I'm nine."

Sam's jaw dropped.

"I'll be ten next month," I added.

He pinched the bridge of his nose. "I should talk to the police."

"You promised!"

"No, I didn't exactly *promise*." He shook his head. "But I said I wouldn't. I won't, I guess." He stood. "Consuelo! *¡Debemos ir!*" He opened the passenger door on the truck. "You ride here. Consuelo is going to ride in the back and tend to Pablo."

"Can't I wait here?"

"Not coming back here. After we get Pablo into an ambulance, I'm heading back to my place." He gestured toward the lowering sun. "Done for the day."

It took me almost as much time to get into the truck as it did for Consuelo and Sam to move Pablo and the stretcher into the back of the pickup, fold the tarp, and stow the camp chairs and ice chest.

He drove pretty slow, because the road—well, calling it a road was reaching. Sometimes it disappeared completely and it felt like he was just driving blindly across the desert, but then the twin ruts would reappear. Other places, going up a grade or down, water had carved deeply into the ruts, and no matter how slowly he drove I was thrown hard against the seatbelt or bounced off the door.

I looked around and saw Consuelo braced in the corner by the cab, shaded by her umbrella. The stretcher and Pablo were secured with straps but Consuelo kept one hand on his forehead, bracing his neck, I guess.

After a half hour we topped a rise and stopped the truck. Sam took a radio mike off its bracket and switched the unit on. "We don't get into range until here." He depressed the transmit button. "Tom—it's Sam Coulton. Got a Hispanic male, dehydrated, some trauma. Got beaten and robbed after crossing south of Bankhead Springs. Was two days without water."

The voice that answered was fuzzed with static, barely recognizable. "You need air evac?"

Sam answered, "Nah. He was conscious when I found him. I've got him on IV fluids and we're less than fifteen miles from Old Eighty. I can meet the ambulance at the Texaco near Desert Rose Ranch Road in about thirty minutes."

"I'll call the sheriff's office. Is he legal?"

"Doubt it. Sheriff for the assault and the INS, if they want, but they might as well send someone to just meet the ambulance at Regional in El Centro."

"Okay—they'll probably dispatch a unit to meet you at the Texaco. Anything else?"

"Nah. Gotta get going if I'm gonna meet the ambulance. Thanks loads. Love to Maribel."

He hung the mike back on the dash and concentrated on his driving. I didn't see how he expected to make fifteen miles in thirty minutes. We were doing much less than ten miles an hour because of the ruts and rocks, but we reached the plain below after five more uncomfortable minutes and turned onto a dirt road that was a highway by comparison. Sam sped up to fifty and we were up to the motorway in fifteen minutes.

"Are those pajamas?" he asked.

I was wearing sweatpants and a T-shirt, what I normally slept in. "Uh, yeah."

"So you were in bed? When it happened?"

I turned away and looked out the window. It was less than a half mile down the road to a petrol station. To my back, he said, "Okay. I won't press but you want to avoid the cops, make yourself scarce while I deal with the deputy, okay?" He pulled into the shade of the pump awning and began rooting under the seat. After a moment he came up with one plastic flip-flop but he had to get out of the car and crouch down before he finally snaked its mate out from under. He took a couple of dollars out of his wallet and handed them and the flip-flops to me. "Go wash up, then get yourself a soda, okay? Until we're done with the EMS."

I was embarrassed. "Uh, thanks so much. I really—"

"Thank me later. Deputy's coming." He jerked his chin and I saw a distant car way down the road. The roof glittered and I could believe it was a police car.

I dropped the flip-flops onto the tarmac and put my feet in them. They were way too big but I shuffled my way into the store and, avoiding the eyes of the woman at the counter, I turned away from the counter to the loo.

The men's bathroom stank and I looked horrible in the

mirror. My hair was matted and there were circles under my eyes. When I twisted around, painfully, the lower edge of my T-shirt was stained brown with a mixture of dirt and dried blood. Fortunately, the dirt made it look more like a particularly reddish mud rather than blood, otherwise, I suspect the clerk would've said something—or even called 911.

I tried rinsing the blood out in the sink but it spread the stain over more of the shirt. I tried the soap dispenser but it was empty, and much as I needed to, I couldn't make myself put the shirt back on. It was wet and filthy and even though there was gauze and tape over the gouge in my side, I didn't want the thing near me.

I dropped it on the edge of the sink and jumped.

I thought it was a very sloppy jump at first—every drawer was out and dumped and the bed mattress flipped over and across the springs. Clothes on hangers were dumped on the floor of the closet. But they were still, not flying through the air. Someone else had caused the mess. I froze, listening.

I wanted to hear something. I wanted to hear my father talking to Mum. The silence was oppressive, weighing down on me like a hot day. Then there was a click and a thud and a whirring sound and my heart beat like a hammer.

Oh. It was the AC cycling on.

I looked out into the hall. More things littered the floors—books, dishes. I began noticing the black powder, almost everywhere. Fingerprinting powder. There were holes in the walls, large, jagged, the edges sticking out, like something had been pulled from the room.

There was masking tape on the floor in the living room, just like on TV, two taped outlines on the floor. And dried blood.

I turned away—flinched away, really. Glancing out glass panes beside the door I saw yellow plastic ribbon stretched across the top of the stairway printed with CRIME SCENE: DO NOT ENTER.

A police car sat at the curb, too, windows down. I couldn't see if anyone was in the driver's seat but there was a crackle after a bit and the sound of someone talking, scratchy, like a radio.

Shite.

I backed up from the doorway, then walked quickly back to my bedroom, the tape on my hip tugging painfully. I picked up a T-shirt, a pair of jeans, underwear, my track shoes, and socks. They'd swept most of the books from my bookshelf, but I found my passport and my hoard, three and a half months' allowance, where I'd left them, stuffed between *Treasure Island* and *Little Big* on the bottom shelf.

I turned to the wall for my sketches, but they were gone. They weren't on the floor, either.

There was a sound from the front, like steps on the stair, and I clutched my things to my chest and jumped.

I was back in the Empty Quarter, by the paintball-splattered boulder, sand and dried grass swirling around me. I heard buzzing, flies returning to the dried blood where it had pooled on the ground. I thought about the bandits who'd attacked Pablo but there didn't seem to be anybody around. I could see footsteps where Sam and Consuelo had carried me away.

I climbed on a rock to change into the clean clothes, easing the pants over the bandages on my hip and brushing the sand off my feet to put on the socks and shoes. It took a moment to visualize the petrol station's bathroom enough to jump back to it. It was the memory of the smell that finally did it. I stuffed the bloody clothes into the rubbish bin, beneath the used paper towels.

When I exited, there was a guy waiting who glared at me. "Shook the door hard enough. What's the matter, couldn't get it open? Is that why you took so fucking long?" He shouldered past me into the bathroom without acknowledging my faint, embarrassed "Sorry."

The ambulance *and* the police were outside. The medical chaps were just easing Pablo off the canvas stretcher and onto the fancy ambulance gurney. Consuelo was watching the paramedics while Sam was just outside, by the store door, talking with a uniformed deputy.

I went back to the refrigerated cabinets and picked out a large bottle of Gatorade, then got some potato crisps. American chips. That's what I miss from England—all the different flavors of crisps. Roast beef and horseradish was my fave.

I paid, using my money, and went out front, away from Sam and the deputy where there was a bench in the shade of the overhang. The Gatorade was good but the crisps were incredible, like my body was craving the salt. I almost went in and bought another bag, but though my mouth said yes my stomach said no. I settled back and sipped from the bottle.

The deputy went back to his vehicle and brought back a map. Sam and he moved up the porch to spread it across the top of a rubbish can. Sam pointed out some specific location for him and I heard him say, ". . . said there were three men. They spoke Spanish to him and each other. Could be a rival coyote gang—I've seen that happen."

"You see any vehicles?"

Sam shook his head. "Only dust. You know, kicked up, but miles away. Normal. Nothing close enough to ID. And I was lookin', too. Didn't want to run into the assholes who did for Pablo."

"Hmm." The deputy tilted back his hat and asked, "You run into anybody out there who wasn't in a vehicle? Someone who just needed a little more water but kept walkin'?"

Sam laughed. "Not today, Ken. The ones who do it right cross at night and hole up during the heat of the day. They may have seen me and Consuelo. I usually don't see 'em at all unless they're in a bad way." He jerked his chin toward the ambulance.

"Okay, then. You going back there?"

"Not today. Goin' home."

"Hmmm. Okay. I'll put the word out to the state police and the border patrol. You run across anything suspicious, let us know, right?"

"Right."

They shook hands and the deputy went back to his car and began talking on the radio.

Sam glanced at me and started to go into the store then stopped. "Huh. There you are. Where'd you get those clothes?"

I opened my mouth to tell him, but what could I say? Really?

"I didn't nick 'em." I stood up and handed him the flip-flops and the two dollars he'd given me earlier. As he took them I dropped back onto the bench, hard, surprised. My knees had given out and it seemed the gas pumps were swaying in the wind. "Whoa."

"Dizzy, eh?" He looked at me a moment longer. "Gonna gas up. Don't really need it but it'll give the deputy time to move off. You just sit here, right? Wish I—oh, well. Just sit. Rest. You feel faint, put your head between your knees."

I nodded.

He went back to the truck. They'd just finished putting Pablo in the back of the ambulance and Sam exchanged a few words with the paramedic before they closed up and drove off down the highway, lights flashing but no siren. I closed my eyes for a few seconds—I thought—then the truck was there, right in front of me.

"Why don't you lie down in back, Griff?"

I wondered if I should go with them at all, but I didn't know what else to do. The thought of lying down was good, really good. I nodded and he helped me climb over the tailgate and drop onto the canvas stretcher. He gave me a folded blanket to

48

use as a pillow. "We're headed west—cab should shade you, takes about forty-five minutes, all right?"

"All right," I said.

He tucked the Gatorade between my arm and my side. I thought about drinking again, but it was too much effort.

I don't even remember him pulling out of the petrol station.

THREE

Burning Bridges

Consuelo lived with Sam, but it was a strange relationship, almost as if she was his girl-of-all-work and he was her little boy. I mean, she cleaned and cooked and did laundry. But she also scolded him constantly, long bursts of rapid-fire Spanish to which he almost always answered, "*¡Claro que sí!*" At first I thought they were married, but she had her own little bedroom in the back with a wall of religious icons, saints, the Virgin Mary, and Jesus.

They stayed at home the day after they'd found me but for the next four days after that, they loaded the truck up with the stretcher and medical supplies and bottled water and drove out.

Consuelo would make me a lunch and show it to me before leaving. *"Ahi te deje listo to lonche."* Then she would say, *"Descanza y bebe mucha agua."* And she would mime drinking from a bottle.

And I would say, *"¡Claro que sí!"*

And Sam would laugh and she would start scolding him again.

I did rest and drank *mucha* water the first day. And slept. It was very easy to sleep. I was tired but thinking about anything—well, about Mum and Dad—exhausted me. It was cry or sleep and sometimes both.

The second day I walked around outside. It was an old adobe house in the middle of the desert, with weathered outbuildings for livestock and horses but they were long gone. The only remotely domesticated animals on the property were a few feral cats.

"They keep having kittens but the coyotes keep their population down," Sam'd told me. "My dad sold off most of the land in the fifties, when he went from ranching to running the co-op in town, but it's been in the family since before the Treaty of Guadalupe Hidalgo. Wouldn't be if they hadn't married Anglos into the family, but that way the land grant stuck. Didn't hurt that nobody really wanted this desert crap."

He said there were neighbors about a mile away, but nobody closer. "Water's iffy. I've got a spring but most places around here you have to drill six hundred feet to get water."

I spent most of the time outside by the concrete tank that captured the spring. The runoff poured over a little notch in the edge and ran down into a gulley—I guess it would be called an arroyo. The little brook didn't last long before it sank into the sandy bottom, but this wet section of the arroyo was a riot of green. Three large cottonwoods shaded the tank for most of the day and if I sat still I could count on seeing birds, jackrabbits, deer, and once Sam pointed at a track in the wet sand and said, "Desert bighorn. Very rare."

The third day I jumped to Balboa Park, on the southern edge near the aerospace museum, and crossed I-5 on the Park Boulevard bridge to get to downtown and the public library on E street. It was a lot cooler in the city—near the ocean and all that—but I still had to rest often.

Outside the library, from the plastic window of a newspaper vending machine, my face stared at me, like they'd put me in that metal box.

BOY STILL MISSING AFTER SUSPECTED DRUG SLAYING.

Drug slaying? I reached into my pocket to pull out quarters to buy the paper but it suddenly felt like every person on the street was staring at me. Instead I turned and entered the library, walked back to the men's loo, and locked myself in a stall.

Drug slaying? That didn't make *any* sense.

Thirty minutes later I peeked out the bathroom door but there wasn't the swarm of police I expected. No one seemed interested in me at all so I worked my way back to periodicals and snagged the *Union Tribune,* then found a chair facing the corner. They'd used a picture from Mum's desk that she took at the zoo three months earlier.

Police still seek missing nine-year-old Griffin O'Conner (see photo) after finding both of his parents murdered in their Texas Street apartment Thursday night. DNA tests of blood found on the site are believed to be the boy's and he is feared dead, but there has been no sign of the boy dead or alive since he was last seen at his karate class Thursday afternoon. Persons with information are urged to contact the police or Crime Stoppers at (888) 580-TIPS.

Large quantities of cocaine found on the premises lead the police to believe that Robert and Hannah O'Conner, UK citizens, were involved in the smuggling and sale of drugs, and that the slaying was either the work of a rival gang or a drug deal gone bad.

Utter rubbish. Mum didn't even like it when Dad had more than one pint at a pub because she'd had alcoholics in her family. Why on earth would the police think—well, 'cause they found the cocaine. And the cocaine wasn't there before, right?

I felt this moment of doubt, a moment of world-twisting alienation, then shook my head. If there was cocaine in the apartment, then *someone* brought it with him, and no matter how many times you see that sort of thing on TV, I doubted it was the police. So it was the murderers, but why?

Because nobody cares what happens to drug dealers.

Because there wouldn't be a hue and cry to find out who did it if the victims were criminals themselves. And the police would be looking in the wrong direction—for other drug smugglers in the city, not for people who'd been following us since we'd lived in England.

I put the paper back, walked between two shelves, and jumped to the elementary school, between the hedge and the stairs, near the flat. I didn't want to go directly there. I was afraid they were still watching the place. If they wanted me, they could be waiting inside for me to appear again. And they'd kill me.

Dead.

Like Mum. Like Dad.

I didn't understand it. I hadn't done anything to them. I was pretty sure Mum and Dad hadn't, either. But they pretty clearly wanted me dead.

I walked toward the flat and almost immediately a woman pushing a baby pram stopped and said, "Aren't you that British boy whose parents were—"

"No, ma'am." The only American accent I could do with any sort of conviction was Deep South. "Ah just look like him. You're the second person who's said that today."

"Oh."

I smiled and walked on but when I turned the corner she

54

was talking on her cell phone. *Bugger all.* I cut into an alley and when the tall fences hid me, I jumped away.

Empty Quarter again. Either I was getting better or I'd already moved so much of the loose dirt here that there wasn't as much to sweep into the air. The bloodstains were fading but ants were now mining the dark dirt. It still reminded me of bloodstains on carpet. I kicked gravel and sand over the spot, ants and all.

It took me a moment to calm down enough to jump back to Sam's place, by the spring. I splashed water over my face and sat down in the shade. After a bit, I wandered back to the house and pulled out the lunch that Consuelo had left me— tamales with pork. The smell made me want tortilla crisps and salsa. Crunchy, salty crisps and a medium salsa—I couldn't handle the hotter stuff.

Why not?

I jumped back to the elementary school. There was a Safeway market a block east of the school grounds and I went there and bought tortilla crisps and salsa and several large bottles of Gatorade, then jumped back to the spring. I started to put the extra Gatorade in the fridge—there was plenty of room—but then I thought about Sam and Consuelo seeing it there so I stashed the bottles under my bed instead. The crisps and salsa tasted good—really good—and I ate them until the bag was empty and I was uncomfortably full.

The bag I buried at the bottom of the rubbish bin, but the salsa jar was half full so I put it at the back of the fridge, behind the pickles and mayonnaise.

I wanted to take another run at the flat, to try to get there without drawing attention, but I was tired and sleepy from the walking and the full stomach. I was still weak, I guess, from the blood loss. I thought about jumping directly back to my room, but I remembered the footsteps on the stair. Maybe they'd planted bugs? Maybe they were watching?

I sat down on the bed. The pillow pulled at me and I slumped over. I was asleep almost immediately after my head touched the pillowcase.

Sam brought home the *San Diego News Daily* and handed it to me in the living room. "They had this at the Stop-N-Go," he said.

They'd used the same photo.

BOY FEARED DEAD AFTER PARENTS KILLED.

The story was a little different but had pretty much the same facts, including the bit about drugs and the implication that Dad and Mum were criminals. I clenched my teeth as I read it.

"It's rubbish, you know, about the drugs. Not in our home—never. Mum had an uncle—he was an alcoholic and he died of it. We weren't very well off—Mum wasn't working because she was homeschooling me, and Dad couldn't get proper work because they're supposed to hire Americans first in his specialty. To make the rent we were stretching every penny of Dad's salary. If they'd been selling drugs, think we'd have to live like that?"

He tilted his head to one side. "I only know what I've read and what you've told me. And you ain't told me much. And what you *did* tell has some, well—what is your name again?"

My ears got hot and I looked away. "Sorry. The newspaper has it right. It's just it was me they were asking for when they came to the door. *My* name. I—" I looked at the wall and squeezed my eyes shut. "They weren't after Mum and Dad. They were after *me!*"

Never jump where someone can see me and never jump near home. I'd done both and Mum and Dad were dead.

"Really. They wanted to kill you?" He raised his eyebrows. "Did you see something you weren't supposed to? Or is there money involved? Do you stand to inherit something?" He pulled a wooden chair from the wall and straddled it backward, arms resting across the back. He gestured at the paper. "This wasn't your average sicko hunting little kids, was it? The paper said the neighbors saw multiple assailants leave, so there was more than one attacker, right?"

I nodded, not trusting myself to speak.

"They came to the door asking for you? Not your dad or mom?"

"Didn't I just say that? It's not inheritance, though. And they weren't coming after me because I saw something I shouldn't."

"Then why? This isn't the Sudan. People don't just kill kids for no reason. Even the sickos have a reason."

57

"It's something I did." It just popped out of my mouth, without thought. My heart raced for a moment but I took a deep breath and said, "It's something I can do."

Consuelo, working on dinner in the kitchen, stepped into the living room and held up a plastic bag with a few pinto beans in the bottom. "Sam! *Necesitamos habas.* Okay?"

He glanced over his shoulder and said, "Okay. *¿Mañana compro?*"

"*¡Tempranito en la mañana!*"

"Okay—first thing." He shrugged and turned back to me. "What do you mean, something you did? You kill their dog or something? Piss in their pool? And you're going to do it again?"

It's against the rules. He'd never believe me without a demonstration. *So why does it matter if he believes you?* It just did. And they were Dad's and Mum's rules and *they* were dead. "Remember at the petrol stop, when you asked me where I'd gotten these?" I pointed at my shirt and pants.

His eyes narrowed. "Yeah. Thought maybe you'd stashed them near the station earlier."

I shook my head and stood up. "Consuelo needs beans."

"Yeah—I'll get 'em in the morning."

I jumped to the Safeway back in San Diego, where I'd gotten the crisps and salsa earlier. I got the twenty-pound burlap bag of pinto beans and paid for it in the quick-check line.

Four minutes after I'd disappeared from Sam's living room I reappeared. The chair he'd been sitting on was on the floor, on its side. He was in the corner, pouring something from a bottle into a glass, but air swept around the room as I arrived and his hand jerked, spilling the liquid. "Dammit!"

I hefted the bag. "Beans."

He stared for a moment then took a gulp from the glass.

I carried the beans into the kitchen and put them down on the counter.

Consuelo looked surprised, then pleased. *"Bueno!"* She rattled off a phrase in Spanish toward the living room and Sam's voice, hoarser than usual, answered, *"Sí. Yo sé."*

I went back in and sat down on the couch.

After a moment, Sam put the bottle away and brought his glass across the room. He picked up the chair and sat on it, forward this time, slumped a little.

"What was that?" he asked quietly, his voice still hoarse. The smell of whiskey came with his breath, reminding me of Dad's weekly scotch.

"I went to a Safeway, in San Diego, bought the beans, and came back."

"I got the bean part. You bought them?"

"The express line was empty."

"Well, yeah, I guess I see that. What I don't get is the traveling to San Diego part."

I nodded. "It's the thing I can do. I jumped. Teleported. Whatever you want to call it."

"Is that how you got those clothes?"

I nodded. "Yeah, I went back to my flat and got my allowance and my passport." My voice broke and convulsively I said, "The tape outlines were still there—and the blood. And someone started to come up the stairs and I jumped away."

"Deep breaths, kid. Slow it down."

I nodded and tried that, until my heart wasn't racing.

After a bit he asked, "How long have you been able to do this thing?"

"I did it for the first time when I was five, back in Oxford. In public. In front of witnesses. We've been moving ever since."

"Moving? Why?"

"Dad and Mum said it was the people who started showing up, asking questions at their work. Then there was a close call on the street—a car. I thought it was a careless driver. Anyway, I skipped back behind a postal box and he missed me but he kept driving. No harm done, I thought. But Mum saw it from upstairs. I heard her tell Dad he'd been waiting for me to cross."

He sucked on his teeth. "Can you go anywhere?"

"Anywhere I've been before that I can remember well enough."

He swallowed the last of his whiskey. "I can see why they'd want you—could be handy. But why do they want to *kill* you? If I could do what you do—if I was the sort of man . . . I'd want to capture you, to *use* what you do."

"Well, Dad talked about that, too. We read that Stephen King book about the girl who is kidnapped by the government."

"*Firestarter,*" said Sam. "Didn't read it but I saw the movie."

"Yeah, with Drew Barrymore. We rented it after we read the book."

"But why not something like that? Why do they want to *kill* you instead?"

My heart started racing and I was breathing fast again. Before Sam said anything I deliberately took deep, slow breaths. Grief may have been one of the things that the gauze was muffling but I recognized the other thing now.

Fear.

They were going to kill me. They followed us for over five years until they found us and then they tried to kill me. Made me want to hide under a bed. Made me want to curl up in a ball and pull dirt over me.

I went back to just breathing. Sam's question still floated out there, though, like a falling glass of milk. You can't grab it in time, you just watch it as it drops, anticipating the spreading puddle of white liquid and jagged glass.

"I don't know why they want to kill me."

Later, after supper, in the dusk after sunset, I told Sam I was going back to the flat.

"Why?"

"Well, for one thing, my clothes are starting to stink. I want my things."

"And don't you think they'll be waiting?"

"Of course!" My voice was shrill and I clamped my mouth

shut and concentrated on my breathing again. I wondered if I was getting asthma or something. After a bit I said, "I'm not going straight there. I'll jump to the neighborhood first and check it out."

"Clothes can be bought, kid."

I dug out my hoard and spread it out on the coffee table. There were sixty-three dollars and some change, fifteen francs, and seven pounds, eight shillings, four p. "Not really gonna last that long, is it?

"Besides—it's my birthday. I'm ten. I should be able to get my own stuff."

"I really don't think you shou—"

Didn't hear the rest but as I walked toward the flat from my jump site behind the school hedge, I felt guilty. I hope I hadn't messed up the living room too much. Sam had done nothing but help me and what had I done for him, besides the bag of beans?

The flat used to be just storage over the detached garage of a small house on Texas Street, but now the house itself was a separate rental property with a front driveway and the yard had been split with fencing. There was a narrow path back along the fence to the flat but there was a police car on the street, pretty much where one had been previously. The cop inside was reading by the dome light.

I backtracked and took to the alley, sticking to the shadows as I got closer to the house and avoiding the backyards with dogs. Fortunately, most of the dogs were inside and the one that wasn't, a big Labrador named Lucky, lived in the rental house in front and knew me. There was a gap in the fence at the corner of his backyard and I crouched and snaked my hand in to scratch Lucky's head. He panted and shifted, putting more of his body in reach. I was working on his upper neck when I felt his ears go up and his head shifted to the right, down the alley. He gave a halfhearted, "Woof!" but then shoved his head back into my hand. After a few more seconds of scratching, I heard the distant scuffing of feet on gravel.

Lucky's fence put me in deep shadow and I was also screened from that direction by an overdeveloped hibiscus growing into the alley from the corner of our yard. Peeking around the hibiscus at knee level I saw the outline of three men walking down the alleyway, backlit by the distant streetlight. One of them carried a shoulder-slung bag and they all walked oddly—lifting each foot from the ground and then putting it down heel first before rolling the foot forward to the toes.

I pulled my head back quickly, afraid they'd seen me, and, in fact, I heard someone say, "What's that?"

Then Lucky began barking up a storm, right by my head. I nearly recoiled out into the alley but realized it was the voice he was barking at.

Lucky's owner, Mr. Mayhew, came to the back door. "Lucky! Get your noisy ass in here!" Lucky went bounding to the back door. "What did you hear?" he said quietly. He put the dog in but stood there on the back porch for a moment, listening. I wondered if Lucky had been barking the night they killed Mum and Dad.

After a moment I heard the door creak again and light silhouetted Mr. Mayhew as he stepped back into his kitchen.

I leaned forward a tad, looking through the branches of the hibiscus. The three men had flattened themselves against the garage door in response to Lucky's barking, but when Mr. Mayhew went back inside they moved again, working quickly.

The stairway from the flat descended toward the street, and at ground level it was visible from the patrol car parked in front. Instead of going that way, the one with the bag set it to the side, then stepped between the other two. They both dropped to one knee and grabbed his ankles, then stood abruptly, throwing him straight up.

He grabbed the railing above and got one foot on the landing with only the slightest noise, then swung over the railing and dropped to a crouch before the door. I presumed the door was locked but he had it open almost immediately. He stood up again and leaned over the railing. The men below heaved up the hanging bag, but he almost missed it, snagging it by the strap at the last minute. One of the men below said, "Careful, you blad!"

"Shhh!" the other hissed.

"Shhh yourself. The detonators would've made a lot more noise than me." I recognized the voice. It was the man with the Bristol accent.

On the landing above, the man disappeared into the flat.

The two men below stepped back into the shadow of the garage door. "What keeps it from blowing up someone else instead—the police, or the landlord?"

"The door sensor. People who come in normally, well, they're not gonna set it off. But if 'e pops in, the motion sensor trips when the door sensor hasn't—see? That'll do 'im a treat."

Like you did for my parents? I groped for a rock—a big rock I could throw or strike with. There was a line of bricks under the edge of the fence, to keep Lucky from digging out. I was able to pull one from the corner, a jagged half brick tucked in to complete the row. I wanted to heave it at them and jump away. Or maybe jump right next to them and hit them in the face with it?

My hands were shaking and I didn't know if it was fear or rage but I didn't trust myself to throw the brick and hit anything.

The guy from upstairs came out and dropped the empty shoulder bag over the railing, then swung over, lowered himself until he hung at arm's length and dropped.

Dammit!

I jumped to the middle of the street and stepped up to the police car. "Hey," I whispered.

The cop recoiled, surprised, his book dropping and one hand going down to his gun belt. "Aren't you—?"

"Yes! But the men who killed my parents are right there!" I stabbed my finger back down the brick path to the stairway. "Behind the garage."

Only they weren't *behind* the garage.

Projectiles shattered the passenger windows and slashed sideways and then the cop was bent over, his head halfway out the window, clawing at the thing sticking out of his neck, a thing with a cable attached to it, and I was in the Empty Quarter in a whirlwind of dirt and brush.

Oh god, oh god, ohmigod. Had they seen me jump? When I appeared at the cop car? But I was on the *other* side, away from them. I'm short—the car should've blocked me.

I still had the brick in my hand. There was blood on my shirt. The cop's blood.

I jumped back to the alley and peered up the path. The three were out by the car, weapons leveled, each looking in a different direction, but they all turned back toward me the instant I appeared.

They know when *I jump.*

They ran back toward the flat and I jumped again, but only down the alley, below my bedroom window. I heard their footsteps by the stairs and I heaved the rock up, hard as I could, through my window.

Fire, light, sound, and flying glass. I couldn't have stayed there if I tried, but I returned to the end of the block almost as soon as I'd flinched away to the Empty Quarter.

Debris was still raining down and the roof was gone from the flat and every car alarm in the city seemed to be going off. I walked carefully up the sidewalk as dozens of people came out of their homes to look wide-eyed down the street.

I backtracked and looked down at the mouth of the alley,

where the men had come from when I first saw them. After a minute, two of them appeared, dragging the third with his arms across their shoulders. As they passed under the streetlight I saw blood on their faces—flying glass, I decided—and one of them smoked, literally, puffs of smoke rising from his hair and shoulder.

A car came up the street and stopped abruptly. They pushed the man who couldn't walk into the back and climbed in on both sides, then the car was moving toward me.

I stepped behind a tree and watched it go by. At the next block it turned right. In the distance, the blare of car alarms was replaced by the rising sound of emergency service sirens.

For a moment I thought about walking back to the flat, to see if there was anything left, anything I could take away, but the neighborhood was well and truly roused and too many of them knew my face.

I jumped.

FOUR

Grasshoppers and Charcoal

When the bus stopped in La Crucecita, I thought it was just another stop in the journey. We'd been five days on second-class buses and *ruteras*—shared minivans in which the other passengers might include chickens and where I'd ended up with a baby or toddler in my lap more than once. We'd stayed one night in a hotel in Mexico City but otherwise it was nap as you could on the crowded, bouncing buses.

Consuelo said, *"Hemos llegado,"* and after five days of hearing nothing but Spanish, I actually understood her.

We'd arrived. I couldn't smell the sea. I couldn't see it. I smelled diesel smoke from the bus. I smelled something involving cattle. I smelled someone cooking onions.

My stomach rumbled. Except for some crisps on the bus, we'd last eaten in Oaxaca, half a day before.

Most of the passengers who'd gotten off at La Crucecita took the street toward downtown but Consuelo led me behind the station and up a forested hill on a trail half overgrown by banana trees and brush. It was humid but not too hot—not like some of the places on our journey where it had taken all my willpower not to jump back to some airconditioned mall.

We crested the hill in less than ten minutes and walked into a breeze that did smell of the sea. Looking between the trees I saw flashes of sapphire blue. Consuelo turned up the ridge, away from the water, but thankfully, still in the breeze. After another five minutes she pointed downslope at a red claytiled rooftop visible between the trees. *"Finalmente hemos llegado!"*

I shifted until I could see more of it around the trees. It was narrow rows of building around three sides of a brick patio. A low wall stood at the open end but there was also construction—additions to both wings were in progress, extending the rectangle.

Consuelo crossed herself and then turned to me. "Wal-Mart. Okay, Greeefin?"

We'd been working on my Spanish the whole trip. *"¡No, acuerdate me llamo* Guillermo*!"*

"Okay. *Lo recordare.* Wal-Mart, okay, Guillermo?"

"Claro que si," I said. *"Un momento."*

The first time I'd jumped in front of Consuelo, she'd gone back to the altar in her room and returned with a vial of clear liquid. She'd splashed it across my face and chest and began a long Latin speech that began *"Exorcizo te"* but that's all I caught, really.

There followed an extremely long argument and discussion between Sam and Consuelo in which she kept using the words *el Diablo* and *demonio,* and he used the word *milagro* multiple times. Finally, to settle it, I had to go into El Centro with her and kneel in the sanctuary of Our Lady of Guadalupe, cross myself with holy water and take communion at Mass, which was probably a sin, since I wasn't Catholic, but she wasn't concerned about sin per se, but *poderes del infierno.*

She decided I wasn't a demon or possessed but she was never completely comfortable about it.

Sam wasn't home but the stuff was waiting where we'd left it, in the old stable—two garden carts (bigger than wheelbarrows) and a large pile of clothes, shoes, toys, diapers (for her grown daughter's newest baby), and tools. I started with the carts, a jump apiece, then began ferrying the rest. Consuelo took what I brought and stacked it in the carts, lashing the resulting head-high stacks in place. It wasn't all bought from Wal-Mart. Just mostly.

It was bumpy but downhill to the house so the issue was keeping the carts from running away from us rather than pushing them. Consuelo's mother, the matriarch of the family, was the first to see her. There were tears and hugs. Consuelo hadn't been home since her husband and son's funeral three years before.

Children and a few adults followed quickly, but most of the adults were at work and the older children were *en la escuela*.

I was introduced as Guillermo, the orphan.

La Crucecita is a village on the south coast of Oaxaca, part of a larger resort area called Bahías de Huatulco, about five hundred kilometers southeast of Mexico City, a couple of hundred west of the Guatemala border. The blue Pacific water reminded me of the Bay of Siam, like sapphires shining in the sun. It wasn't that crowded, compared with Acapulco or Puerto Vallarta, but being a gringo, I wouldn't stand out that much, because of the tourists. That was the theory, explained by Consuelo through Sam.

Her extended family worked for the resort hotels as maids, gardeners, busboys, and cooks. Those who didn't work for the resorts were in the U.S., sending money back, but this was changing as the resorts grew and entering the states became harder.

There was a welcome-home fiesta that evening and Consuelo handed out presents for one and all. I would've been lost except for Alejandra, one of Consuelo's many nieces. Besides Spanish, she spoke English, French, and German, was twenty-five and beautiful. She'd been working in the tourist industry since she was sixteen and had attended the Instituto de Idiomas in Mexico City. She ran a translation services agency and taught weeklong immersion classes in Spanish, working with the resorts. "Visit beautiful Huatulco, lie on the beach, and learn *español*," she said. She smiled often with her eyes but when her wide mouth opened into a grin, it was staggering.

It took me five minutes to fall in love with her.

We spoke in French, not because her English wasn't excellent, but because she had less opportunity to practice French. That was a little difficult for me—Mum and I would speak in French.

She introduced me to everybody from Señora Monjarraz y Romera, Alejandra's grandmother and Consuelo's mother, to her many cousins' children. I was given name after name, but only held on to a few. The food was both familiar and strange. I ate a tortilla filled with guacamole and some delicious, spicy crunchy thing.

"What is it? Uh, *qu'est-ce que c'est?*"

Alejandra's eyes were alight. "*Chapulines . . . los saltamontes.*"

I looked confused and she tried French. "*Les sauterelles.*"

It took me a minute. "*Les sutere*—GRASSHOPPERS? I'm eating grasshoppers?" I unrolled the tortilla and it became all too clear she was telling the truth: legs and all, fried, from the looks of them.

She laughed. "If you don't want them, *I'll* eat them." She reached out.

Stubbornly, I rolled them back up and ate the rest of it. *Crunch, crunch, crunch.* It was still delicious but knowing . . . I didn't go back for seconds.

The next day I had *la turista,* really bad, with a fever and cramps and the groaning, stumbling run to the toilet over and over. I wanted to blame the grasshoppers, but no matter what else I thought, they'd certainly been cooked well. Consuelo brought me a bitter tea to drink. When I asked what it was, she said something in Spanish and added, *"Para la diarrea."*

Grasshopper tea, no doubt.

Later, she brought a small wooden box and burned it by the window in a metal pan. When the charcoal had cooled down she mimed eating it. *"Comete el carbón de la leña."*

"Yuck! Absolutely not."

Alejandra came and coaxed me into taking it. "It absorbs toxins and is the quickest way to stop the diarrhea. You only take it this once. No more after. That would be bad for you."

"I don't want to. You also eat grasshoppers!" I set my teeth and curled in on myself, prepared to resist to the death. But she didn't play fair.

"Faites ceci pour moi, mon cher."

French, dammit.

"For her." I managed half of the charcoal washed down

73

with some salty boiled water. "For electrolytes." And they stopped bothering me.

The runs did stop after that and I was able to eat rice with chicken broth that evening. Two days later, after my first fully solid meal, Alejandra and Consuelo took me out to the patio and we sat in the shade of the banana trees growing near the wall.

"My aunt tells me that you are not just an orphan, but that those who killed your mother and father are still after you."

Reluctantly, I nodded. I knew we had to tell her. It wasn't right to ask her to help without knowing. But I *liked* her. I didn't want her to push me away, to not want anything to do with me.

"And she brought you here to avoid them. They would still kill you if they could find you."

"Yes."

"She won't tell me why they want to kill you. She says only you can tell me."

"Ah." I licked my lips and nodded to Consuelo. *"Gracias."* To Alejandra I said, "That—that was good of her." Consuelo was keeping my secret.

Consuelo said something then, and there was a brief back-and-forth between her and Alejandra that was too fast for me to follow.

Alejandra looked back at me, a little confused. "She says she is willing to try that thing. The thing she said she didn't want to do before."

I raised my eyebrows at Consuelo. I knew what she was

74

talking about. I'd suggested it back in Sam's living room, where he could translate, but she'd been afraid. I guess the thought of five more days on buses and *ruteras* was more daunting.

And it would certainly answer Alejandra's unspoken question.

"When does she want to leave?"

Compared with the stuff we arrived with, Consuelo's little suitcase was tiny, but she was taking back a box of regional foods she couldn't buy in California.

"Any grasshoppers? *¿Chapulines?*" I asked.

Alejandra laughed and Consuela said, "No. Sam no like."

Still, walking uphill into the jungle, the box was heavy and I was sweating by the time we reached the level spot where I'd transported Consuelo's gifts. I could've jumped here from the patio but I was cautious. I'd decided that the rules had some merit.

So what about rule four? Who tells you when it's okay to jump?

"Can you keep a secret? Like your aunt?" I used English. I didn't trust my French and it had to be crystal clear.

Alejandra tilted her head to one side. "Will it hurt me? Will it hurt my family?"

I swallowed. "*Not* keeping it could hurt your family." She frowned and I said, "*I* would never hurt them, but those who are after me might hurt them, getting to me."

"Okay. I can keep a secret." She leaned slightly closer to

me than her aunt and whispered, "And who tells their parents *everything*?"

Ouch.

"All right. Let's start with this box."

I jumped to Sam's living room. He wasn't in there but I heard movement in the kitchen. I called out, "Sam, it's Griffin."

"Jesus!" I heard a dish clatter across the bottom of the sink. He appeared in the door, wiping his hands with a dish towel. "Everything okay?"

"It's fine. These are Consuelo's," I said, raising the box slightly. I put it on the table. "She changed her mind about the traveling thing."

"Oh? You guys someplace private?"

"You ever been there?"

"For the funeral."

I stared at him. "I didn't know you knew her then."

He shrugged. "Just. I found them. Their bodies."

Oh. "Well, we're in the jungle, up the hillside from the house."

He nodded.

"Okay, then. I'll be back."

Alejandra was sitting on Consuelo's suitcase, her head between her knees. Consuelo was fanning her with a hat.

I knelt beside her. "You okay?"

"*¡Jesús Cristo!*" She sat up. "*Mi tia dice*—my aunt says you just traveled to California."

76

"Verdad." In the week I'd known her, I'd never seen her lose track of which language she was speaking.

"And back again?"

"Yeah."

"How?"

"Beats me. Can I have the suitcase?" I pointed.

She stood up abruptly and Consuelo steadied her.

I took the case and jumped.

Sam was sitting in the corner, arms crossed. I put the suitcase down against the wall.

"What took so long?"

"Alejandra."

He frowned, then said, "Consuelo's niece? Is she there?"

"Yeah. Only her, but we didn't tell her first. Only asked for secrecy. She's a little freaked."

His eyebrows went up. "Well, it do take some getting used to."

I jumped back. Alejandra flinched but it didn't seem to be fear. Just the sudden appearance of something unexpected, caught from the corner of your eye.

"So, you're going to take my aunt now?"

"That's the plan."

"Have you ever done this before, with a person?"

I shook my head. "When we were discussing it, back at Sam's place, I tried it with a kitten. Worked fine."

"My aunt is larger than a kitten. How do I know you won't leave part of her behind?"

77

"That's just gross," I said. But it worried me a bit. The heaviest thing I'd carried was the carts we'd used. They only weighed about thirty-five pounds, though, big as they were.

Alejandra said, "Try it with me first."

"What?"

Consuelo, watching us both carefully, said, *"¿Qué dijisté?"*

Alejandra pursed her lips and I realized she didn't want to tell her aunt, that Consuelo would protest.

I stepped up to Alejandra from behind and put my arms around her. I only came up to her shoulder blades; my cheek pressed against her spine through the thin cotton of her sundress. She smelled *wonderful*.

Consuelo said something sharply and took a step toward us. I jumped.

I staggered a bit, but we were both in Sam's living room.

Alejandra gasped and staggered, too, and I steadied her— kept her from falling over. After a moment she said, "Uh, Guillermo, you can let go."

"Ah." I stepped slightly away from her, then caught her again as her knees buckled.

Sam and I helped her sit on the couch.

"Where's Consuelo?" said Sam. "Is everything all right?"

"You explain," I said to Alejandra, and jumped.

Consuelo was talking fast and furious with lots of gestures and I couldn't get one word in ten, much less meaning. Well, I didn't understand the sentences but I sure understood the sentiment.

I kept trying to calm her down but finally I just jumped behind her, like playing tag with Dad in our exercises, put my arms around her, and jumped.

We both staggered forward in Sam's living room, but Sam steadied Consuelo and Alejandra grabbed my arm.

Everyone was a little wide-eyed, even me.

Deep breaths.

"You know," I said, "I'm hungry!"

Consuelo couldn't stand for anyone to "have hunger." She didn't even need it translated.

We ate out by the spring and Alejandra marveled at the dryness of the air and the trees and the rocky brown hills.

"¿Dónde está lo verde?" she asked her aunt. Where is the green?

Consuelo got a stony look on her face. *"No tenemos agua, ni hay verde."*

I realized what she was thinking about: her husband and son. No water, no green.

Alejandra realized it, too. *"¡Oh, perdóneme! No pensé."* I didn't think.

Consuelo waved her hand. *"No es importante."* She said something else that I couldn't understand.

Alejandra translated. "She's glad she doesn't have to spend all that time on the buses. Even if it was terrifying."

"Travel Air Griffin. When you absolutely have to be there today."

"Greefin? Why Greefin?"

"Uh, that's my name. My real name. Consuelo and I chose Guillermo because *they* know my real name, the people who killed my parents. And Griffin is unusual. So, it's Guillermo, okay? I mean, you can call me Griffin in private, I guess."

"No," said Sam. "Go on as you mean to go on. She calls you two different things, it's easy to get mixed up. She calls you one thing, then she's not likely to make a mistake in front of someone else."

Alejandra nodded. "True. But going on? Are we meaning to go on?"

Sam switched to Spanish, asking Consuelo something, and the conversation broadened to include all three of them, but I didn't follow it. I was watching Alejandra. Waiting. Hoping.

Finally, she turned to me and said, "Well, Grif—Guillermo. Do you want to live with me in La Crucesita? I have a small house behind the Hotel Villa Blanca, just across from Chaué Beach. There is a small room above the carport with spider-webs." She shuddered. "But it could be cleaned out."

I nodded solemnly.

"You'd have to study hard and learn *español* because I'd be telling everyone you are a distant cousin on my mother's side, the Losadas. She's from Mexico City, not *de el lado de mi familia de La Crucecita*. And you would have to go to the beach often, to tan, so people would not call you *el gringito*."

I nodded more vigorously. "All right. I'll work hard and I'll keep up my homeschooling. And I'll learn Span—*español*. And I can shop for you, in the United States if you want, or Thailand, or Lechlade, uh, our village back in Oxfordshire—in England."

"Whoa, boy," said Sam. "You are going down to Oaxaca to disappear, not draw more attention to yourself."

My ears got hot and I stared at the table for a moment. "Uh, right."

Alejandra reached out and touched my arm. "I'm sure you will be a big help to me. You already speak French and English. Learn Spanish and I can put you to work in my agency. Or I'll find you work as a guide. Not to worry. But school will be your main job, *comprende*? Guillermo Losada?"

"*¡Claro que sí!*"

"*¡Excelente!*" She smiled again. "I have an appointment this afternoon. We should return."

And so it went.

Alejandra, who was afraid of spiders (*las arañas*), had me do the initial clearing of my new room. Once all the webbing was down and the screens were covering all the windows, she pitched in with hot water and lemon-scented cleanser. By the end of the week I had a cot, a dresser, and a small table (with bookshelves above) for a desk. A metal folding chair completed the suite. It wasn't air conditioned but the sea breezes made it quite comfortable.

I had very little to put in the dresser but that changed over time and, really, in the warm climate of Las Bahías de Hua-tulco, I didn't need much.

Alejandra not only began as she meant to go on, calling me Guillermo and never referring to me by my real name, but she also stopped talking to me in anything but Spanish, miming verbs, pointing to objects and naming them. Very rarely she would illustrate a complicated verb conjugation by comparing it with French usage. She towed me along for the immersion classes she ran at the resorts, too.

It took me three months to learn enough *español* that she began talking to me in French and English again. Three months later, she considered me fluent and it was another three months before I stopped sounding like a foreigner. By the end of my second year, most locals thought I'd been born in Oaxaca. I still looked European but so do many Mexicans without *indio* ancestors.

I worked for her agency half days, for which she paid me off the books. Three hours a day I worked on schoolwork, in English *and* French *and* Spanish. Spanish word problems for math. European history in French. Sciences in all of them. And I sketched, everywhere.

I was "that boy who draws" to everyone—in the park before the church, at the marinas, on the beach. Most of it stayed in my sketchbooks but the wall of my room slowly accumulated the drawings that worked.

The nightmares were bad at first, but they slowly lessened in frequency. Twice, in that first month, I woke up, my heart pounding, staring around in the sandy wash of the Empty

Quarter, that spot in the Sonoran Desert where Sam had found me, bloody and unconscious.

The Spanish study helped. At least there was something to do when I woke up. I'd finished *Don Quixote* and was working my way through Arturo Pérez-Reverte's books about Capitán Diego Alatriste. Or, I'd do a unit of math. Math was always good.

But it was probably a year before I slept all the way through the night.

In my second year there, I bought a boat, a little fiberglass dinghy with oars, a daggerboard well, and a small, removable mast with a lateen sail. When I got it, there was a hole in the bow as big as my head and the sail was in tatters and there were no oars, no rudder, no daggerboard, and no life jackets. I spent a week running errands at the Santa Cruz Marina, translating, running to the store, and acting as a local guide. At the end of that I had the oars, two life jackets, a stained but intact Sunfish sail, and enough fiberglass and resin to fix the stove-in bow. I made a daggerboard and rudder out of cheap lumber, scavenged from construction sites, and fiberglassed it.

Alejandra had doubts. "You could drown!"

I raised my eyebrows. "I suppose, if I were knocked completely unconscious, I could. But not from a cramp or being tired, no matter how far out from shore I was. Think about it." After a bit I added, "My dad and I used to sail, in the Bay of Siam. It was a bigger boat."

She registered it in her name but it was really mine.

There are nine bays and thirty-six beaches in the Bahías

de Huatulco, many of them unreachable by road. I explored all of them—swimming, fishing, snorkeling—as well as the edges of the jungle.

More than once I got caught in the surf, which can be very rough, and I was rolled, though luckily, I'd unstepped the mast and lashed it, and I was able to recover the oars and the life jackets and the daggerboard. Later, I learned how to time things, to ride the breakers in and to row out without taking on too much water.

Rodrigo, one of Alejandra's many cousins, teased me about the sail and oars. He wanted me to buy an outboard, but I hated the stink and the noise. Every time he brought it up, I rubbed my fingers against my thumb. "*¿Tu tienes dinero para la gasolina?*"

He was always broke so he had no answer. He'd reached the magic age of fourteen and what little money he had went to *las niñas,* the girls. While I took him out fishing and lobstering, sometimes Alejandra forbade me to lend the boat to him, to impress the girls.

"*You* might not drown, *mon cher,* and I know Rodrigo can swim like a fish, but his girlfriends? Let him get his own boat. I don't want him sailing off to remote beaches. He'll get them drowned, or worse!"

I didn't quite see what was worse than being drowned, but I figured out what she meant, eventually. It seemed odd, since she had boyfriends and there'd been times when they'd spent the night.

She blushed when I pointed this out, but she said, "I am not fourteen or thirteen. *That* is the difference."

Rodrigo's answer to this prohibition was to try to get *me* to take him *and* his *filles du jour* out, but the dingy was too small. I offered to take these girls for rides *sin él*—without him—but this didn't go over so well.

Every three months I climbed the hill into the jungle behind the Monjarraz compound and jumped to Sam's place in California. Usually I would just transport Consuelo and some gifts back, but once Sam came, too, and I took him fishing.

I had my eleventh birthday, and then my twelfth.

Pretty much I kept the rules. I didn't jump near Alejandra's house or anywhere near people. If I wanted to practice, I'd take my boat out at sunrise and sail to the Isla la Montosa, a rocky island east, out from Tangolunda Bay. I could usually get in an hour before the dive boats showed up with the tourists.

I was being *careful*.

So I really resented it when they still found me.

FIVE

Going to Ground

I had ten minutes' warning—an enormous amount of time, really. Didn't even have to jump. Not immediately.

I was at the translation agency, Significado Claro, answering phones for Alejandra while she attended a real estate purchase at the lawyer's office down the block. An American couple were buying property for their retirement.

They had a bit of *español* but wisely wanted to be absolutely clear on everything they were signing.

Our dentist, the elderly Dr. Andrés Ortega, called and asked for Alejandra. I explained she was out and offered to take a message. He asked for me, that is, Guillermo Losada.

"*Es yo, Doctor.*"

He spoke rapidly in Spanish. "Some foreign men were just here with an agent of the AFI. They had dental records. Your dental records." The AFI was the Agencia Federal de Investigación—the Mexican equivalent of the United States' FBI. "They were American records and they had a different name on them . . . Guillermo." He paused. "I had to give them your address. They just left here."

My heart began pounding like waves crashing into the shore after a storm. *Ka-thud. Ka-thud.*

Traitor teeth. I'd had two fillings eight months before. See what not flossing will do?

"Do they have the address of Alejandra's agency?"

"No—it wasn't in your records. I didn't show them hers."

"Thank you, Doctor. Thank you very much."

I hung up. My impulse was to jump away, to Sam's, but Dr. Ortega's office was in Santa Cruz, the next village over. It would take them at least ten minutes to get into La Crucecita and then they would be going to the house.

So I jumped to the house first. I kept my money in a Oaxacan black pottery hexagonal box, the lid decorated with cutout triangles. I think I liked the box better than the money.

I dropped it in the middle of my bed, on the light spread.

Then the contents of my dresser, grabbing the drawers, dumping them on the spread, and sticking them back in the dresser. It took three armloads to strip the books off my two shelves.

I took the corners of the blankets and pulled them together. The bundle was almost as big as me but it still came with me when I jumped it to Sam's broken-down stable in California. I jumped back and grabbed the sheets and the raincoat hanging behind the door and the corkboard that held a few drawings, some snaps of Alejandra, a picture of Rodrigo with one of his girlfriends, and a picture of me sailing my boat. These, too, went into Sam's stable. Then I was back, pulling the sketches off the walls, tearing out the corners where they were tacked up. I carefully put these in Sam's stable, on the pile.

They'd taken all my pictures last time, when they killed Mum and Dad.

When I jumped back, the room looked weird—uninhabited. I wished I could put dust all over it, so they'd think it was abandoned months before, but I didn't know how to manage that.

I used the house phone to call Alejandra at the lawyer's office.

"*¿Bueno?*" she said when they called her to the phone.

"*Te amo.*" I'd never said it before, but I did. As if she were Mom, or a sister.

"*¿Guillermo, que estas loco?*"

"*No estoy loco. Veniron y deboir.*"

She switched to English. She wasn't understanding me

but it wasn't the words, it was the situation. "Who has come? Why must you—oh. Oh, no!" She'd got it. *"¡Ve rápido!"*

"Don't go home. They'll be watching." I hung up the phone and walked out the back door.

Five minutes later I was on the patio of the Hotel Villa Blanca when they pulled up. I had a newspaper covering my face, and I'd ordered a *limonada* to justify my presence. The paper shook in my hands and I had to brace my elbows against the table to stop the movement.

They drove by in two cars, one after the other, eyeing the house casually. One car parked up the street, the other pulled into the hotel's drive, not forty feet from where I sat.

It was all I could do not to jump away, but I realized they were there for the same reason I was—you could watch the house from here. The plates were Oaxacan and it was *not* a rental. The driver, a man in a rumpled white suit, looked Mexican. His passenger wasn't.

I'd last seen him in San Diego, the night the flat blew up.

My hands, for some bizarre reason, stopped shaking.

I shifted my chair slightly, letting me see through the archway to the registration desk. I couldn't hear them but Martín, the desk clerk, was shaking his head. The man in the white suit took his wallet out of his jacket and flipped it open, showing the clerk something. I saw Martín's eyes widen and then he picked up the phone and spoke into it.

Señor Heras, the manager, joined them from the office. After another moment's discussion, Vidal, the bellman, was summoned. They unloaded the trunk, only three pieces of luggage, but one piece the man from San Diego grabbed out of the trunk as Vidal reached for it.

"I'll get that," he said, loud enough that I heard it across the lobby. "Fragile." He still had that Bristol accent. I wanted to jump, away, mostly, but I remembered the night they killed the police officer in the street by the flat. They'd seemed to know when I jumped without seeing me.

I watched them take the stairs up while Vidal rolled his cart back to the freight lift. When they were out of sight I wandered back to the front of the hotel. Standing just inside the door, I could see the other car down the street, parked on the other side, where they could watch the front of Alejandra's house.

Vidal came back after a minute. "How did they tip?" I asked him in Spanish, rubbing my fingertips.

He made a face. *"Los mezquinos."* Cheapskates.

"What side are they on?"

He jerked his thumb to the left, toward Alejandra's. *"En la planta tercera. Al fondo."* He pointed to west. *"¿Por que preguntas?"*

"Because they are looking for me." As I said it, I felt my face twist and I knew I was on the verge of tears. I took a deep breath and steadied myself. "So, you don't know me, okay? I'm leaving but we don't want them to hurt Alejandra, right?"

"¡Claro que si!"

Everyone who knew her thought highly of Alejandra.

"I owe you."

He jerked his chin up and grinned. *"Claro que si."*

At the edge of the beach park, vendors had tables selling Oaxacan souvenirs to the tourists—black pottery, Guatemalan clothes, painted wooden carvings made with tropical hardwoods. I found a small hand mirror set in painted copal wood for twenty dollars americano. I paid for it without haggling.

Vidal unlocked the back stairs of the hotel for me, to access the roof. It was a popular place for the employees when the resorts over at Tangolunda Bay did fireworks, so I'd been there before, but I didn't jump.

I didn't want to jump around them—not until I left for good.

The roof was gravel over tar and I took my time moving across. I didn't think they'd be able to hear me through the roof, but all the rooms had balconies and if they were out there, or had the sliding door open, they might.

As I approached the concrete parapet that edged the roof I heard them talking. From the sound, they weren't on the balcony but they must've opened the door.

My Bristol-accented friend spoke: "—'e won't be the owner—'e's just a kid. We should find out who owns the house, and all of 'em that lives there." He groaned, surprising me.

"Your stomach, still? It happens sometimes, to foreigners. Different bacteria, they say." Mexican-accented English. Probably the man from the Agencia Federal de Investigación.

"Bugger the bacteria."

"I will ask downstairs who owns the house."

"No! They're neighbors. You ask questions, they might answer, but they also might pick up the phone, *comprende?* There must be records you can check more discreetly."

The agent of the AFI said, "Yes, there are records. Over the phone is not so good, though. With my badge in their face, the results are better. You will not need me directly?"

"No. It's a waiting game now. Call me." I heard the door open, but before it closed I heard him add, "And please get me some Pepto-Bismol." It was a strain. This man clearly wasn't accustomed to saying please.

"Of course, Señor Kemp. And some more bottled water?"

"Good of ya."

The door closed.

"Shite!" I heard him—Kemp?—groan again and then move. His footsteps changed, echoed.

He's in the bathroom.

I heard his belted pants dropping to the floor and the un-mistakable sounds of gastric distress.

Impulsively I shoved the mirror into my back pocket and swung over the parapet. It wasn't a hard climb at all. The di-visions between the balconies were honeycombed bricks pro-viding good foot and hand holds. Heights didn't bother me, since I could always "jump" to safety. I was on the balcony before he flushed the toilet. I knelt in the corner and silently edged one of the chairs back to partially hide me.

There were footsteps and he came to the edge of the door-way, binoculars held to his face. He was scanning the house, Alejandra's house, *my house.*

No. Not my house, not my home. Not anymore.

Maybe I could push him off the balcony.

He checked the street; he checked the windows of the house. He took something from his pocket and, still looking through the binoculars, he spoke into it.

"Anything?"

There was an answering voice, crackling with static, low volume. "No. Not since earlier, when we were driving over here from the dentist. Felt maybe seven jumps in a minute."

"You've got better range than me—I only felt two of those, at the edge of town. I sent Ortiz out to find out who owns the house. Keep your eyes open, right? I can't watch continuously."

The response was too low for me to hear, but this side of the conversation was loud and clear: "'Cause the bloody toilet is not line of sight with the target, okay?" He put the radio back in his pocket and, groaning, turned back to the bathroom.

I'd been right to climb down.

Range. Varying range. One of them could sense me from, say, Dr. Ortega's office, five kilometers away, but Kemp couldn't. But, say he felt my last two jumps right before I called Alejandra; they could've been in La Crucecita, within one or two kilometers, but still taking five minutes to find their way.

He'd certainly feel it if I jumped while on the balcony.

Then the realization came. Range. They could sense jumps but they couldn't have been practicing on me alone. They had experience sensing jumps. Other jumps. Not mine.

Mon Dieu, there are other jumpers!

Kemp groaned again, the sound echoing off the bathroom tiles. I remembered that time I was sick shortly after arriving in Oaxaca and wished I could just die and get it over with. I hoped he suffered for weeks.

I used the mirror then, when it was clear he was still on the toilet, scooting to the edge of the doorway and tilting it, low, to peer into the room. Their suitcases were in the closet, just sticking out, but that briefcase he hadn't let Vidal carry was on the bed. Wonder what it contained.

Well, why not find out?

It was just a step inside, on the carpet, silent, but I think the light was dimmed very slightly as I went through the door. Even sick as he was, Kemp noticed. I heard him scramble for his pants but I had my hand on the case before he cleared the bathroom door. He was trying to point something at me, something bigger than a gun, bringing it up, but I jumped.

Dad's voice—*Don't let anyone even* point *a weapon at you.*

No, Dad. Do my best.

Didn't go far.

Couldn't. If they weren't chasing me, they'd turn their attention on Alejandra. So I wanted them to chase me.

I went to the island in the next bay over, the Isla la Montosa, a rocky bit slightly less than three hundred meters across, only a few hundred meters off the east headland of

Tangolunda Bay. It had a tiny spit of land extending toward the mainland that sheltered a bit of beach less than fifty meters long. The rest of the island was big waves on rock shore with a raised brushy interior.

It was only four kilometers from the hotel.

They should have felt it.

Felt, but could they track it? Did they feel the direction? Would they come?

The briefcase had two three-digit combination locks and they were engaged. Two sets of a thousand possible combinations, solvable, I suppose, with enough time and patience. Just start at 000 and work your way up to 999.

I sat on the little beach and hit the locks with a rock, which not only opened it eventually, but greatly relieved the tension while I waited, especially when I screamed as I did it.

Every few minutes I'd take a break and jump to the four quarters of the compass, the east, north, south, and west shores of the island, to see if they were coming yet, and with the jumping, let them know I was still here.

The suitcase popped open eventually but it flared bright and hot and I had to throw it away from myself. I was surprised I hadn't set it off earlier, with all the banging, but it was only meant to self-destruct, not designed to kill, clearly, or I'd be dead.

The contents were ash and melted plastic and blackened metal. There was a charred corner of a passport, but it was the most recognizable thing I found. The flare had been *really* bright and the afterimage floated in my field of vision.

Magnesium, maybe. That had been one of the more memorable homeschool science experiments—the thin ribbon of metal that went right on burning after Mum dropped it in the water.

They came in two boats—one that went directly to the beach, avoiding the rocks that dotted the mouth of the cove, and another that tried to do something on the seaward side. They could have landed a swimmer but it would've meant writing off the boat to come any closer to the jagged lava. The waves would've smashed it into the cliff. In the end, that boat, too, circled the island and put in at the cove.

There were only three of them—Ortiz from the AFI, Kemp from Bristol, and a bearded man who towered over the other two. He hadn't been at San Diego, I would've remembered a man that tall.

That meant they'd left someone at the house.

Maybe more than one. Don't assume you saw them all.

I thought about Alejandra, then, and the rest of the Monjarraz family. I wanted to go check, but nothing would lead the bastards to her—to them all—faster than me jumping there.

Phone, I thought. Later.

Meanwhile, I had questions.

They had fishing poles and an ice chest. I felt my ears get red and my throat got tight.

Did they think I was *stupid*?

I don't know why this made me so mad. Hell, it would probably have been a great deal of help if they thought I was some dumb kid.

I watched them from the higher part of the island, where the brush began, just inland from where the spit that formed the cove joined the main part of the island. I was sitting down in the shade, having found a flat rock to park my arse on. Except for the sandy beach, every place else I'd sat on the whole island seemed to consist of poky bits of lava.

I wondered if they knew the difference between someone jumping to a spot versus jumping away or if it was all the same to them. It's not like they sensed me when I wasn't jumping, or I'd never have been able to get onto that balcony.

They left Ortiz by the boats, with one of the rods, and they headed down the beach, toward me. They also brought fishing rods, carried in their left hands, but their right hands stayed close to the bags slung over their right shoulders. I jumped ten feet to the right, my eyes watching them.

Both of them reacted, looking right at where my head now poked above the brush . . . but Ortiz hadn't flinched a bit. He was still pretending to fish from the beach, by the boats.

Ah. He doesn't feel it. They do.

I turned around and ran briskly off, straight up the middle of the island. Well, straight as the brush and boulders let me. The shrubs tore at my shirt and I ended up with a few scratches on my bare forearms but I was probably doing better than them. They were bigger and would have to force their way through and they'd dressed like tourists.

Shorts, for God's sake.

I was out of line of sight in thirty seconds. They'd still been working their way up the rising rock at the end of the beach—not quite a cliff—but not something you go up without grabbing a handhold here and there. I pushed on until I was at the far end, right at the edge of a real cliff. There was a boulder that stuck up a bit from all the rest and I climbed up its backside and peered over. I needed the visual cues— the waves hitting the cliff below drowned out any chance of hearing them move through the brush.

They came, Kemp right down the middle, like I'd come, but the other man, the big one, came along the cliff's edge, from the right. He'd come quickly and I guess there wasn't as much brush to fight through, but he'd also come along the edge.

I jumped right there, *right* beside him, and he flinched off the edge. I didn't have to touch him but he almost snagged me, going over the edge; he was so much taller, his clawing hand whipping through my hair as I stepped back.

He didn't land on the rocks, though it was only a matter of luck. A wave hit just before he did, and he was kicking and splashing, head mostly above the water, as he washed back out over the tide pools at the bottom of the cliff.

One.

If I'd hesitated, Ortiz would've been warned. His radio was crackling as I brought the rock down from behind, and Kemp's voice said, "Ortiz, look out!" as Ortiz dropped to his knees. I'm sure it's a *crimen federal* to strike an agent of the AFI. I didn't succeed in knocking him completely unconscious but I had his own handcuffs on his wrists before he was able to do more than moan.

I towed the second boat away from shore with the first, making a bad job of it going out between the rocks. My boat cleared but a swell swung the second craft into the rocks and scraped paint and fiberglass down the side.

Too bad. Maybe they'll lose their deposit.

I dropped the anchor in the lee of the island, halfway between it and the headland opposite. It was deep there, over forty meters, but by using the anchor line from both boats, I was able to reach the bottom with some line to spare. It would drag, though, if there was any change in the wind.

Que lástima.

Even in the sheltered lee of the island, the pitch of the boat, especially jerked up hard by the anchor line, was making me ill. I jumped to the opposite shore where a two-hundred-meter beach called Playa de Mixteca was tucked into the east side of the headland. Its north end was bordered by a beach pavilion but I went to the other end and looked across at the island, only two hundred meters, two soccer fields, away. I could cross back instantly, but Kemp would be a while if he tried to reach me. He'd have to swim at least as far as the boats.

I spoke into Ortiz's radio.

"Mr. Kemp," I said. "Are you there?"

"Who is this?" He didn't know my voice and he wasn't certain, but he probably suspected.

"It's the orphan." That really said it all. They probably

had my name. Names. But I wasn't going to hand them anything. I just needed to know *why*. "How's the tummy? Still got the squirts?"

"Griffin," he said. "You made a mess o' things."

"Ortiz was conscious when I left."

"Bit o' concussion. Might hemorrhage."

"Hard luck. What about the big man?"

"He's pissed."

"And wet?"

"Oh, aye." He paused. "What you want, boy?"

There it was. "I want to know why. What did my parents ever do to you? Why did you kill them? Why are you trying to kill me?"

He paused, then said, "Don't know what you're talking about." The carrier cut off with a hiss of static.

"Kemp?"

No answer. I tried a few more times, then swore and switched down through the channels.

Kemp's voice: "—to the map, it's Mixteca beach, got it?"

"I'm moving."

"Good, we're going to quarter the island. He might have a base. Or a supply depot. Had to have some reason for being here."

I wanted to transmit: *To lure you gullible assholes away from people I care about.* But that would just tell them to go after Alejandra. Instead I pushed the button down and said, "Best of luck with that, wankers. I'm leaving this town—I ever see any of you again, I'll do more than hit you with a rock."

I tossed the radio in the water.

I wanted to check on Alejandra, but I jumped away to Sam's ranch, sat down by the spring, and ground the heels of my palms into my eyes.

Consuelo checked on Alejandra for me, long distance. She was going to call her directly but I said they might trace that call, so she checked through one of her other nieces.

Alejandra had locked up the agency and, in the dark of the night, joined her current boyfriend at the Santa Cruz marina.

A sixteen-meter sailboat, laying over on a trip from California to Florida via the Panama Canal, left that night, having acquired needed expertise in local waters and language.

"Good," I said. *"Muy bien."*

I was still furious. Two homes gone. But she was safe for now and that lifted serious weight from my shoulders.

"What are you gonna do?" Sam asked. "Seems like jumpin' is just gonna bring 'em down on you."

"And if I don't jump, they also come after me. They didn't find me by my *jumping.* It was my teeth. My dental records. I can jump all right. Just can't be around people when I do. That is, when I jump *to* a place. Doesn't hurt to jump away around people. Don't care if they know where I *was.* Just where I am— where I stay, where I live."

Sam considered this for a while. "Okay. I know some places people don't go. Places that are too rough, too hot, no water."

I nodded. "That's the right idea. But not a place you know. Better you should be able to say, 'I don't know where he is.'" I kicked at the floor. "They could still trace back to Consuelo from her family. If they tried hard enough. It's too many people to keep a secret."

He frowned at that and glanced toward the kitchen where Consuelo was cooking dinner. "Fair enough. Think on it, though. There are places you can go where no one else can, right? I mean, once you've been there? Think on that."

The INS came for Consuelo two days after I left Oaxaca.

Her green card was good—she was ostensibly employed by Sam at over 125 percent of the mandated poverty line— but someone said she was actively engaged in smuggling illegal aliens into the country.

I watched this from the old stable, my fist clenching and unclenching. I thought about jumping into the dusty driveway and snatching her back to Oaxaca, but that was probably no safer. Sam, knowing where I was, held his hand behind his back and shook it side to side.

Later, after they'd left, he wandered back by the stable but didn't come in. He talked to the air.

"I knew the agent in uniform but those two in the suits— never saw them before, and I've met most of the local boys. I think you might want to take a hike, after dark, down the spring wash. There's an old backpack up in the hayrick—I'll leave some food and a canteen by the spring. Walk a long way before you jump, right?"

"What about Consuelo?"

He spat in the dirt. "They'll either deport her or not. I really think they're trying to flush you. *¿Sabe?*"

"I could pull Consuelo out."

"And then they'd *know,* wouldn't they? We know some pretty high-powered immigration lawyers. I'll get them on it."

"Shit!"

He spat again. "Yeah. Shit and shinola. But you'd only make it worse."

I spent the afternoon packing my clothes and my money and a sketchbook. I hid the rest of the stuff under an old feed trough.

I walked three hours, briskly, heading south. I'm pretty sure I was at least six miles away, but I kept walking, anyway.

Where was I to go? They had to have people down in Huatulco. They might still have people around Sam's place. Probably someone in San Diego, but I had lots of places I could jump to there. They couldn't be everywhere, could they?

How many of them were there, anyway? I meant the ones who could actually sense when I jumped. I had no idea. A secret organization can only get so big before it stops being a secret, right?

I slept on a bit of sandy ground between two south-facing boulders. I used the bottom of the backpack, the part with my clothes in it, as a pillow, and the boulders were still warm from the day's sun.

In the morning, after eating and drinking and a pee against a rock, I felt better. I walked another three miles before I decided I was far enough.

I jumped to the east, back to the Empty Quarter, a place I was pretty sure was clear. There was a sheltered crack up the ridge, not big enough for me, but big enough to hide the pack in. It wasn't easy to get to—wasn't too high—but there was nasty jumping cholla all around it. I could jump past the spines to a ledge below the crack, and shove the pack in where it was pretty much invisible.

I jumped into San Diego, my old place under the hedge at the elementary school. I figured there was a chance they had someone within range who had felt me arrive, but the odds of them being right there seemed pretty slim.

I figured I was safe, especially if I got out of the neighborhood quickly. It took me a half hour to walk across Balboa Park and into downtown, to the library.

I found what I wanted in a book on mining history. It was in the desert east of the San Diego Mountains—the Anza-Borrego Desert State Park. Getting there took me two days.

I started by jumping onto a Greyhound bus while the driver was still examining the boarding passengers' tickets. I sat in the row before the toilet, hunched over, making myself even shorter than I normally was. Fortunately, the bus was only half full and no one wanted to sit near the loo.

The bus was westbound for Tucson and El Paso, but I left it at the turnoff for Plaster City, just west of El Centro. The bus didn't stop there, but it slowed on a slight hill and I was gone.

I considered hitching from there, but I wanted no trace of my presence in the vicinity—nobody who could remember my face. I worked my way toward the little town after once jumping back to San Diego for Gatorade. Took me two hours to walk the seven miles.

Plaster City gets its name from the U.S. Gypsum plant there. They make wallboard and ship it east and west on regular rail but the interesting thing was the twenty-seven-mile-long narrow-gage railroad they operate to reach their quarry in the Fish Creek Mountains.

And *that* was where I wanted to go.

I rode one of the empty gypsum haulers up the line and used my T-shirt across my face to keep from breathing the dust. The crusher was up at the quarry and even though they'd dumped the hauler at Plaster City, the swirling dust was still something awful and I kept thinking the doors in the bottom of the car would swing open and dump me under the wheels.

When we got there, I walked away from the quarry, up a ravine, then jumped back to Sam's and had a long shower, but I was still sneezing up dust that evening.

The next morning I went back to San Diego and changed

all my pesos to American at Baja Mex Insurance & Currency Exchange. Next I took the crosstown bus out to a Home Depot and bought rope, flashlights, batteries, and a hard hat. Then it was back to the Fish Creek Mountains.

There were several old mines farther up in the mountains, most of them with danger signs and blocked off by welded steel grates put up by the park service.

Obviously the grates gave me no trouble but most of the mines went back only a little bit, useless to me, or had caved in after a mere twenty feet.

The one that worked was more extensive, a copper/gold mine long abandoned, but much more developed. That one had a vertical shaft, though the platform holding the steam-powered lift had long rotted away. An old iron ladder, though, still went down the side, and once I jumped past the grill, I chanced it. But I was prepared to jump, if it gave way.

A hundred feet below, horizontal shafts followed played-out veins. One of these had broken through into a natural cavern, perhaps sixty feet across, and air moved from the cavern into the shaft. At the far end of the chamber, a rivulet of water flowed out of the rock face, splashed down through a series of sink-sized basins, and then flowed out again through a crack at the base of a flowstone wall. There was a natural passage that dead-ended in a smaller chamber but the air flowed out of fist-sized cracks near the water wall.

This was good. This would do.

I wasn't out of money yet—I would've been glad to buy

the stuff—but there was no way the gun shop would sell a kid smokeless powder. Hell, they didn't even want me in the shop. As soon as they saw me, they asked, "Where's your dad, son? You here with an adult?"

I had a choice of getting mad or getting sad.

"Wrong door," I said, and left.

I got furious.

It helped to be mad at them. Made it easier to do what I needed to do.

They had massive locks and pull-down bars to close the shop up. And this affected me how? I cleaned out their supply of smokeless powder, fifty-three metal cans. Dynamite would've been more efficient but that required detonators and all that, and I didn't know where to get it, much less how to use it.

I stacked the cans in the horizontal shaft leading to the cavern, but at the end next to the old lift shaft. I concentrated on four of the timber pillars supporting roof beams. I used a can opener, punching a hole in each one of the cans. The second-to-last can I laid on its side, and the very last can I used in my best pirate-movie fashion, pouring a trail of powder that ran from the mouth of the can on its side to thirty feet down the tunnel.

Didn't know it would burn so *fast*.

My intention had been to jump to the surface, to listen to the explosion, but I flinched away to the Empty Quarter instead, and missed it.

107

The air was full of dust and chemical smell when I jumped back into the cave, worse than my trip in the gypsum hauler, so I left and didn't return until the next day.

I examined the horizontal shaft from both sides. Rubble had dropped from above, mostly filling the bottom of the lift shaft. My tunnel was completely filled and the others mostly blocked. From the other side, the tunnel had collapsed back to the next roof beam, about fifteen feet of fill. It wasn't totally blocked, for a breeze still drifted out that direction, but it was certainly proof against people sneaking up the tunnel.

There is something very wrong when being in an underground cavern with no exit is the safest place to be.

SIX

Old Paths

I tried over the course of several days, but it didn't work. Finally, I returned to the San Diego library and found the image I needed in a UK tourist guide.

The Martyrs' Memorial in Oxford sits where Broad Street meets St. Giles. The guidebook reminded me of what it was for, but Mum never told me the gruesome details. The martyrs were three Church of England Protestants burned during the bloody reign of Mary.

Burned . . . gross.

How could people do something like that?

The picture, though, brought me back—literally. It reminded me enough of the place. Horrifying memory, actually. One second I was there with Mum, waiting for Dad to snap the picture, then a car came out of Broad Street way too fast and slammed into a taxi not ten feet away. Horns, glass, screeching rubber, buckling metal and folding plastic. Noisy.

Scared me all the way back to our flat in Lechlade.

Instantly.

But I had no memory of that flat. You'd think I would, but I can't even remember what my room was like.

It was raining in Oxford and cold, and the pedestrians walked by hidden under their umbrellas or hunched into their bright yellow macks like turtles.

I crossed the street and walked, carried along in the stream. I was getting wet and cold but I didn't mind. It had been ninety-two degrees Fahrenheit at Sam's and I appreciated the chill. At least for a while. When I got too cold and too wet, I picked a jump site near Blackwell's Bookstore on Broad Street, but walked on several more blocks.

It was my new rule. Don't arrive from where you left. You don't know who might be waiting. I turned a random corner, brick and flats and a mini-grocery, and jumped.

It was something I learned from recent experiments in

shopping. If you jump as you turn a corner, and somebody sees you, it's okay. If they were watching from behind, they think you just continued around the corner. If they see you from the other side, they think you stepped back.

People flicker out of our sight all the time, through doors, around corners, onto subways, but we fill in where they went. We know that the body is still there just out of sight, on the other side of the door, in the receding subway, around the corner.

But Kemp and his lot—they knew better.

Had to warm up a bit at Sam's. My new place is damp and dark—a bit too much like Oxford on a rainy night—but Sam's at seven hours diff from Greenwich was hot, bright, and arid. A half hour in the sun dried me right out.

I called the cavern the Hole, less like a Hobbit hole and more like a badger's den, where the dogs had hounded me, gone to ground.

It was comfortable, slightly damp, slightly cool—the kind of place where you wanted slippers and a cardigan or maybe a fuzzy dressing gown to keep the chill off. The chamber was lit around the edges with low-voltage landscaping lights. I had a few brighter lights, also low-voltage, near the bed and the desk; I only turned these on when I needed them, but the landscaping lights stayed on all the time—there were no windows, no sunlight touched the Hole. Last thing I wanted to do was fumble around for a light switch when waking in the night. Sure didn't want to jump into that blackness.

The whole lot was run off a bank of boating batteries that stood on a shelf down the old mining shaft. During the day, when sunlight hit the mouth of the mine and warmed all the surrounding rock, an updraft pulled air out through the rubble in the collapsed tunnel, causing a palpable breeze in the Hole. At that time I could run the petrol-fired generator to recharge the batteries, since the smelly exhaust fumes flowed out through the gaps and cracks.

Only had to run it once a week or so—really overdid it on the batteries.

I nicked them.

I nicked the generator.

I nicked the lights, too.

Hell, I stole everything these days.

I hated to think what Mum would say.

The gunpowder I used to blow the mine tunnel was the start, of course. I justified it—they would never have sold it to me—but it didn't take long at all to run out of money. The batteries alone would've wiped my savings.

The batteries came from a marine supply place in San Diego, down where the jets heading into the airport thunder overhead and it seems like you can count rivets when you're done ducking. I don't know what I looked like. Maybe a bit dirty, a bit furtive, but one of the floor clerks followed me around as I checked off the stuff on my list. Batteries, Deep Discharge Gel Acid, pretinned battery cables, a three-bank automatic battery charger, and the generator.

They had it all, I hadn't pulled anything off the shelf, but

I was careful not to linger in front of any of the stuff I was looking at. I asked a bunch of questions about their self-furling headsail gear and then bought a small anchor for my dingy.

I hadn't left the dingy in Oaxaca. I could just pick up the hull if I first removed the mast and the rudder and the dag-gerboard and oars. It sat in the Hole, upside down, all of its accessories stacked neatly around, the life jackets spread on top. My boat in a cave with no exit, in the middle of the desert.

They had a monitor at the checkout counter, one of those things with a four-way split, showing the counter, the door, the emergency exit, and the counter where the marine elec-tronics were. They didn't seem to be monitoring the batter-ies or any of the other stuff on my list.

Batteries are *heavy*. I took twelve that night and, since I'd emptied it, I took their sturdy display shelf, too, and the rest of the stuff from my list.

I wore gloves.

The furniture came from Ikea. The bed, the desk, the book-shelves. That was easy. Assembling them was easy. Getting them level?

Stupid cave.

Home Depot "donated" concrete and a level and a mortar mixing tub and the stuff I needed to level sections of the floor. They had lots of cameras but their own shelving blocked them. If I crouched under one of their racks, I could jump un-observed, even during business hours.

The batteries were heavy, but ready-to-mix concrete is heavy, too. I could barely move the eighty-pound sacks but they jumped okay, and when I was mixing I tore them open and used an old coffee can to scoop the mix out.

It was ugly when it was finished, rough, coarse, but it *was* level. My futon bed sat level. The desk was level. The three bookshelves were level. The dining table was level, but looked weird. It could sit four but I'd only taken one chair.

I mean, after all, why did I need more than one chair?

But it bugged me and bugged me and finally, one night, I jumped back into Ikea and completed the set.

Of course that bugged me, too, but at least when my eyes passed over the table I didn't flinch anymore. It was the right number if I ever wanted to bring Sam, Consuelo, and Alejandra there.

It took Sam five days to get Consuelo out of detention. By the end of it, a border patrol supervisor was facing an official investigation. He was unable to account for a large deposit into his bank account around the time he'd ordered her arrest.

"One of his own men tipped the lawyer," Sam explained. "I'm not sure if he was pissed because his boss took a bribe or because he didn't split it."

We met at the Texaco petrol station where we'd met the ambulance. I'd jumped in four hours before, even before it opened, and waited in the brush, with a book.

Consuelo told me there was a new bellman at the Hotel Villa Blanca, a foreigner—meaning a Mexican from the north, not an Oaxacan—who took his breaks where he could watch Alejandra's house and in his off time walked in the hills above the family compound, with binoculars.

Alejandra had found an old schoolmate from the Instituto de Idiomas who wanted a change and was willing to take over the translation agency. Alejandra took a job on Saona Island in the Dominican Republic, translating for English- and French-speaking tourists, and studied the local *caribeño español,* switching her *l*'s and *r*'s with abandon.

Consuelo *tsked-tsked* about the boyfriend who returned to Huatulco "still friends." Too much closeness had finished the relationship and I was glad until she told me that Alejandra was seeing someone else, a Dominican local.

C'est la vie.

They dropped me in El Centro and drove home. I jumped back to the Hole from there, a good hour after they'd left.

There's a field in Oxfordshire nowhere near the Thames or the hills or historic ruins but it is a few miles away from a village train station on the Reading line twixt Oxford and London. There's a bull there, too, but he's with his cows so he's pretty calm, except when I pop out of thin air right next to him. Even then, he usually just snorts and shambles away.

Mostly in the rain.

At least it seemed that way. Picking my way between the

cow patties through the damp grass, letting myself out the gate, and then slogging along the asphalt to the station was a good walk, but it was a bit damp.

More than once, I showed up in the pouring rain and jumped to the station directly. But it really had to be unpleasant for me to do that.

All it took was one of *them* to be riding through on the 9:52 to Paddington Station and they'd be waiting for me in the field one foggy day.

Enough to give one nightmares.

It's not that I wouldn't jump into London or Oxford proper, occasionally, but if I did, I hurried away from that spot as quickly as I could.

I wanted the run of the place.

I wanted the world.

Phuket was easier than Oxford. My memories were stronger, the smells, the unbelievable colors of the ocean, the Portuguese-influenced architecture. I bought garlic sausage, sticky rice mixed with banana and shredded coconut or red beans wrapped in banana leaves from vendors carrying their wares in rattan baskets. Or satay sold from stainless steel carts pulled by motorbike.

I was running out of money.

I could've earned it, I suppose. Translating, perhaps, in Spain or France, but I was just a kid, and a short kid at that. Without someone like Alejandra to steer work my way— well, it would've been a hard scrabble.

But still it took me a while to get up the courage.

My first attempt would've been a miserable failure if it hadn't been for the fact they didn't even know I'd been there. I saw the armored-car guards (one of them the driver) leave the locked vehicle right outside the Safeway and head in with their canvas bags. I walked up to the other side, peeked in the thickly armored window, walked back between two vans, and jumped.

The truck was empty. This was their first pickup.

I took an assembled bicycle from Wal-Mart that afternoon and filled the tires. The next day, I followed the armored car as it meandered through that neighborhood going to three grocery stores, two jewelry stores, and then the Horton Plaza Mall. It took them multiple trips at the mall, back and forth

I made my move when they made their next stop, servicing an ATM at a Henry's Marketplace.

Didn't have to move close—I'd seen the inside of the truck the day before.

Good thing I'd been moving batteries and cement bags. I cleared out the back of the truck in under five minutes, jumping back and forth to the Hole.

Had to cut the bags open.

Three hundred thousand dollars. Give or take twenty thousand.

It was one of the big security companies. Surely they had insurance?

Mum would not be happy. Nor Dad.

Well, they're not here, then, are they?

———

The tourists drove me out of Oxford—them and their buses. The buses are the oddest thing. The companies run them and the tourists use them to get from place to place, but it's more like a city bus, running all the time, and mostly empty.

I hate diesel fumes.

I found a karate dojo in Knightsbridge run in conjunction with a fancy gym. It was expensive and I had to fake my dad's signature on a release, but they had a really nice locker room with *showers*. I paid for a year.

It was my birthday present to myself—I was thirteen.

I'd had it with cold sponge baths in the Hole, but the local solution called for more construction, maybe a propane water heater, and let the soapy water flow away with the clean under the flowstone wall, but I hated the idea. I pictured some desert spring where the bighorn sheep came to drink, foaming up with soap suds. It was the reason I used a bucket toilet odorized with pine-scented disinfectant back in the smaller chamber and, when I needed to, dumped it at one of the park's picnic area pit toilets late at night.

I was still careful. I certainly didn't jump anywhere near the dojo. I used the Underground a lot, jumping to lots of different stations, always trying to pick a place, before I left, that I'd never jumped to before. Also someplace the video-cameras didn't cover—where phone stalls or info signs made a blank spot.

Leaving, going back to the Hole, I just jumped from the moving subway, whatever train came. I'd either pick a mostly empty car and jump when no one was looking, or I'd move to the next car, jumping when I was between the doors in the noisy, rattling space.

But having classes to go to was good; it meant I had a schedule, a structure that I didn't have before.

It meant I had to buy a watch.

It was one of those time-zone clocks, showing the time in two different places at once. I kept it on U.S. Pacific Time, minus seven, and London, Greenwich zero. If I hit a button it would show me the time in Phuket—Greenwich plus seven.

Breakfast, cereal, I tended to eat in the Hole. Got a little twelve-volt fridge to hold the milk. Eight o'clock in the morning and it was time for the four o'clock afternoon teen class at the dojo. I wasn't the youngest one there, but I was the shortest.

But I made up for the lack of size.

"Fierce 'un, eh?" That's what the senior instructor, Sensei Patel, would say to Martin, the junior instructor who had our lot, after watching me spar. I was swathed in pads and usually picking myself up, yet again, but I was right back in there, punching and kicking.

"Not right, that one," Martin would say, a big smile on his face. He knew I could hear. He was just teasing. "Oi! Less blocking with the head, there."

After class I'd drop off my laundry (done by the pound), usually yesterday's clothes and the day's practice *gi* and the linens every week or so.

Lunch was whatever, usually in London, without jumping. Sure it was evening there, but if you want a particular type of food and you can't find it in London, you aren't trying very hard. Well, except Mexican, perhaps. I ate Indian, Chinese, and the occasional bit of fish and chips.

There was a library branch not too far from the dojo where I'd do my homeschooling workbooks. I was still working through the French science series and the Spanish math so the ladies who worked there kept coming up to try out their *"Bonjour, mon ami"* and *"¿Como esta?"*. They were a bit disappointed when they found out I wasn't so foreign, but they were always good for a pointer or two when I got stuck on a bit of math or a bit of chemistry.

Reference librarians, they explained, lived to answer questions. And I was a nice change from the kids who wanted them to tell them "where the reports are kept" or came to snog in the stairwell or score some weed back by the toilet.

Dinner might be anywhere. Morning in Phuket, something in San Diego. Not London, though—getting past midnight in London.

Sometimes I'd just jump my dingy down to Bahía Chacacual, a bay twenty miles west of La Crucecita, and I'd skin-dive for my supper, lobster or fish, cooked on the beach with limes and peppers.

Then home to Hole and hearth and up again, pick up my laundry and repeat as needed.

After six months, Sensei Patel said I could come to evening adult classes. They tested me for *nikkyu,* low brown belt, after that and I passed, barely.

Didn't really like forms, the kata. Didn't see the point, so I didn't practice them as much as I should.

"Well, then," said Sensei Patel when I expressed this opinion, "you're a right git, aren'tcha?"

He sat me down on the floor and said, "Watch."

He did the first two steps of *Heian Shodan,* a lower block and a stepping midlevel punch. He paused between the block and the punch. "That's how you do it. Now, come here and attack me. Front kick."

I got up and did my best kick. He blocked it to the side with the lower block and the knuckles of his fist brushed my nose and I fell backward, overbalanced. Hadn't even seen him step in but he had. For the barest second, I wondered if he'd jumped.

"How do you think I learned that? Made it mine? It wasn't from sparring. Now—watch." He did the whole kata, but this time there was a different rhythm and intensity to it. Block-punch, block-block-punch. He didn't even move that fast but everything flowed from one to the other.

"You want to spar better, you get on with your katas, eh?" He tapped me on the forehead. "Use a little imagination. You think you're out here by yourself but that's not what it's about. Enemies surround you. Start acting like it."

Ouch.

Every couple of months I'd give Sam a call, using a pay phone. I'd talk in Spanish and ask for Carlotta or Rosa or any of a bunch of different names. If he said *tienes el número in-correcto* and hung up, we'd meet the next day down the road from the Texaco, on a rise where you could see for miles. If he said, *"No la conozco,"* I'd have to postpone—he couldn't make it the next day or he felt like it wasn't safe.

But this time it was okay and Consuelo and he sat on their folding chairs and I perched on the tailgate and we ate a nice curry and spoke in Spanish.

"Alejandra is coming home," Consuelo said. "She said to tell you she misses the *chupulines*." She smiled briefly but she was clearly worried.

"Is the bellman from the Villa Blanca still around?"

"Oh, yes. Mateo buys drinks in the bars for my relatives. He's been letting Rodrigo use his car in the afternoon to drive around the girls."

"¡Estúpido! Did no one tell him?" I wanted to go slap Rodrigo around. This stung. I thought he was my friend.

Sam shrugged. "Tell him what? Anything Rodrigo knows Mateo can find out from anyone. Someone tells Rodrigo don't talk to Mateo and suddenly Rodrigo *does* have a secret. Leave well enough alone. It won't last. Rodrigo's mother is forbidding it—he doesn't have his license—and she told him she'll have cousin Paco arrest him if he doesn't listen."

"He never listens," I said. "What about Alejandra? I'm worried."

Consuelo sighed. "She misses her family. And she broke up with her boyfriend, the Dominican."

"I could—"

"What?" Sam said. "You could show up and give them a reason to bother her?"

I dropped off the tailgate and kicked a rock. It flew over the edge of the hilltop, then crashed through the mesquite and cholla. My big toe throbbed and I tried not to limp as I stepped back to the tailgate.

"Right. What about you guys? You think this is safe?" I waved my hand around at the empty hillside. The highway was seven miles south of us and the dirt road running out to the hilltop was clearly visible and empty, a thin straight line that didn't bend until it hit the bottom of the ridge.

Sam shrugged. "As safe as it gets without no contact."

Consuelo shook her finger at me. "You are not a jaguar to live alone and solitary. It is unhealthy." She reached out and plucked at a hole in my jeans. "More like a coyote. But even coyotes keep together, eh?"

"Okay. I'll go howl at the moon. Maybe go through the trash cans."

Sam tapped his plastic fork against the Styrofoam container. "This didn't come from any trash can. Where did it come from?"

"Huh? Oh, Café Naz in the East End." At his blank look I added, "London."

"Ah." He mouth worked for a moment but nothing came out. Finally he said, "Not bad. Not bad at all." He poked a finger toward my upper torso. "You look healthy. Whatcha doing for exercise?"

"Karate. A dojo in—well, maybe I shouldn't say where."

"Right. Not if you go there regular. And income? You got enough money?"

I looked away. "No worries. Don't have to worry about the rent. I'm saying my prayers and washing behind my ears and brushing my teeth, Papa." Teeth. I didn't want any more X-rays compared if I could help it. "I'm even doing my lessons. I'm up to Second Form, uh, tenth grade in the science and I'm starting precalculus."

"What is that, four grade levels ahead?"

I shrugged. "Whatever." I tried to be indifferent but it was nice to have someone make a fuss. Quite nice.

It made me afraid for them.

I waited thirty minutes after they left, watching the dust trail of the pickup all the way to the highway before I jumped away to the Hole.

Jumped to Embankment Station at the curvy underground part, not the aboveground platform, in a nook, behind a crowd of tourists, and someone started screaming.

Someone was shouting, "MOVE! MOVE YOUR BLOODY ASS!" The two women tourists in front of me were holding their hands above their head, cameras dangling, and one of them was screaming. Over their shoulder I saw someone running up the platform holding a big, oddly shaped gun— one I'd seen before.

He fired and something smacked into the wall on both sides of my nook and suddenly the two women tourists were thrown into me. I heard the breath leave their lungs and they stopped screaming, but they were spasming and I smelled ozone. I wasn't pinned—though the women were jammed across the opening of the nook there was still room behind me—and I jumped.

"Wait!" I yelled. I don't know why or to whom, but the sound echoed in the wash of the Empty Quarter. I jumped immediately to Charing Cross platform and stepped onto the northern train heading back toward the Thames and Embankment Station.

Nobody screamed and nobody shot at me but my eyes were wide open.

It took maybe three minutes for the train to reach the other station, but he was gone. There were transport police on the platform. They'd gotten the women out of the nook and seated on a bench. The cable was still there, taut between two areas of broken blue tile, so I guess they wiggled back into the nook and ducked under it. I didn't get off the train and as it left, we passed more transport police in the tunnel itself, flashlights waving as they searched.

I got off at Waterloo and took the Jubilee line back to Green Park, then took the Piccadilly line over to Knightsbridge. I wasn't even late for class, though it seemed as if I should be.

The next one was closer.

Elephant and Castle Tube stop and he was more careful than the last guy. He followed me and didn't attack until we were in the twisty stair up to street level. He was firing up the stairs and I heard something mechanical click right before he shot, so I was bending forward and looking back. The cable tore overhead and tangled in the handrail above me and I was standing in desert sand before the next one arrived.

Right, then.

The first one was clearly not just coincidence. They were watching the Tube stations.

I jumped back into London, on the other side of the Thames, to South Kensington Station. It was only one stop away from Knightsbridge but I didn't get on the train. I wandered between platforms—there are three different lines at that station—keeping my eye on everyone else. It was busy but when I stayed on the Piccadilly platform through three different train arrivals, the faces had all recycled.

I took the stairs up to the eastbound platform then took the passage under Cromwell Road over to the Natural History Museum. I spent an hour there, wandering back and forth between the whales and the dinosaurs, checking everybody who came near. All random faces. Finally, I walked up Brompton Avenue to Knightsbridge, picked up my laundry and a bite of falafel, and hopped a cross-city westbound bus.

The falafel was fresh, warm, crisp, and it sat in my stomach like a dead weight. How many of them were there? How many stations could they watch? Were they going to force me out of London like they'd forced me out of San Diego and Huatulco?

What the hell do they want?

JUMPER: GRIFFIN'S STORY

Somewhere past Ealing Common, when the bus was mostly empty, I jumped back to my Hole.

I got my hair bleached. Bought a reversible jacket and three hats. Bought some dark-framed glasses with clear glass. Still used the subway, but I was very, very careful. Never jumped to a station. Never left from a station. Tried to choose a new arrival point every single day, but never near my departure point for that day.

I definitely stopped jumping into the cinemas without paying.

I passed my *ikkyu,* upper brown belt, test. Sensei Patel said my kata didn't suck nearly so bad now. I'd actually tagged Sensei Martin in the ribs with a front kick during the sparring test.

And I made a friend.

SEVEN

Punches and Pimples

Henry Langsford was an upper-class twit with a sense of humor. We'd tested for *ikkyu* together and he always gave me a hard time about the Americanisms in my language and my accent. His father was a second secretary at the British embassy in Amman so Henry was at a boarding school in London. "But all they have at school is boxing. I do that, too, but I've received dispensation for this."

He was long and thin, pushing six-two, even though he was my age. He could reach me with a kick long before I could strike him, but I was faster. But the boxing was something. I tried to stay away from his hands. I'd go outside for a kidney or sweep his foot, midkick.

Henry suggested a cuppa. "Won't be in trouble until half past nine and 'tis only seven stops up the Piccadilly line. You for it?"

I had a dozen excuses on my tongue. Instead I said, "Why not?"

We hit Expresso Bar on the north side of Beauchamp Place. He got tea, I took a double-shot latte loaded with sugar.

"No wonder you're so short. Stunted your growth, you did, with that caffeine. How do you sleep?"

It was actually midday still, for me, but I said, "Maybe that's why I'm faster than you."

We walked back to Brompton Road and into Hyde Park and wandered a bit, tending east.

We talked about travel, places we'd lived. We'd both been to Thailand, both been to Spain, but him in the south, Cádiz and Seville, and me in the north, Barcelona and Zaragoza. I talked about the "colonies" and Mexico. He talked about Kenya and Norway and family vacations in Normandy. That led to speaking in French and he was oh-so-superior about his accent—my County Durham origins corrupted the purity of my pronunciation, but my vocabulary was bigger.

129

"Et où est votre maison, mon petit ami?"

"Little? I'm not ducking through doorways. And I lives in an 'ole in the ground."

"What? Like a Hobbit?"

"Very like an 'obbit."

"A basement flat?"

"You could say that. On the west side." Of America.

He considered this. "Your feet are a bit hairy."

"So, your home would be in Rivendell, eh?"

"Huh? Oh, right. Elves." He chuckled and looked at his watch. "Oi. Bugger me—I'm going to be talking to the Head if I don't get a move on."

We were close to Hyde Park Corner Station and he dashed for it, his long legs flashing. "Kick you in class," he called over his shoulder.

"In your dreams!"

A cuppa after became a regular thing, and when I turned sixteen the dojo went up to Birmingham to participate in a tournament. Henry and I roomed together, under the supervision of Sensei Patel.

"You never talk about your folks," Henry asked, on the train up.

It came out of left field, that, and surprised me. I blinked. "Bugger, something in me eye." After a deep breath I said, "Whatcha want to know? Dad teaches computers. Mum teaches kids their Voltaire and Beaumarchais and Diderot, in the original. Awfully boring if you ask me, but they're all right." I was tired; I woke and slept on Pacific Coast time and here I was floundering around at 9.00 A.M., Greenwich zero. It felt like two in the bloody morning.

"Seems like they're pretty handy with the ready," Henry said. "Dad's always on about the fees at the dojo, but in that proud sort of way. Nothing but the best for mine, don'tcha know. You don't seem to have any problem."

I shook my head. "Well, that's not their money—that's me own."

"Rich grandmother?"

"Distant uncle." Uncle Truck. Armored T. Truck.

I was eliminated in the second round of brown belt *kumite* by a college-aged brown belt from Coventry, and then Sensei Patel and another instructor protested.

"What?" I said, as Sensei walked past me to the judges' table. "He beat me fair and square!" He'd scored to my face with a lightning-fast roundhouse kick.

The judges listened to Sensei Patel, then called my opponent over. There were some heated words and then the referee came back on the floor and announced I'd won, by forfeit.

My opponent gave me a murderous look and left.

Sensei Patel explained. "Saw Mr. Wickes, there, take his *shodan* test five years ago. I've seen it before in these big regional tourneys. People dropping a belt level so they have a better chance of placing. Like a third-year college student retaking his A-levels. What's the point?"

131

Huh.

I made it through two more rounds and then was eliminated by a kid from Paddington who didn't even block my attacks. He'd just strike at the same time, leaning this way or that to avoid my hand or foot. Three quick points and out.

"Could learn a lot from that 'un," Henry said. Henry hadn't made it past the first round.

We watched the Paddington *karateka* go on to take first, so I couldn't feel too inferior.

Sensei Patel required all of us to participate in the kata competition and I was surprised to take second in the brown belt category. "See?" Sensei said. "Look what happens if you apply yourself a bit." He ruffled my head. The trophy was half as tall as me. It would be a bear on the train.

"A monument. That's what it is," said Henry. "A monument to your greatness."

"To perseverance," Sensei suggested.

After, Sensei checked in with us before he went out to eat with some of the judges and *his* sensei, over from Okinawa. "You lot all right by yourselves?"

"Of course, Sensei."

"See you after at the hotel, then. No later than ten, right? There's a dance, if you want, or there's the cinema over on Broad Street, right?"

"Right, Sensei."

We changed, dropped our *gi*s and the "monument" in the hotel. Henry was now calling it a "monument to your perverseness." We found a pub where the food wouldn't be "too

132

healthy." Henry's choice. "S'all we get in dining hall. Veggies, veggies, veggies. With a salad."

Fish and chips were duly ordered and destroyed.

"But this greasy food is going to have me all out in spots, you know," Henry complained after, not a crumb left on his plate.

"And that would change things exactly how?" I was having a bit of trouble with pimples myself but Henry's was a spectacular case, a patchwork of trouble spots that he called his map of Africa. "Anyway," I said, "if you're still getting pimples with all the veggies they're shoveling down you in hall, then I don't see how a few chips are going to make it worse."

Henry swiped my last chip. "Look who's drowning his troubles," he said, jerking his head toward the adjoining bar.

It was Wickes, the disqualified black belt from Coventry. He was sitting in a booth with a half-full pint and two empty mugs. He glanced up and our eyes met. I dropped my eyes and turned back to Henry. "Oi. Guess Mr. Wickes is past eighteen, then."

"Why do that? Lie about your rank. What's he get out of it?"

I shrugged. "Maybe he has a trophy shelf to impress the gels." I glanced sideways briefly, just a flick of the eyes. "He's still looking at us."

"Umm. Well, it's going to be some time before I'm ready for pudding. Let's see what's going at the cinema."

"Suits."

133

We'd already paid but Henry put down a tip for the bar-maid, saying, "Buy yourself one." She laughed at him and I was teasing Henry about it as we cut across the park toward Broad Street.

Wickes was there before us. "Think it was funny, do you?"

I stopped dead. The green was bright enough, from all the lights at the arcade, but there wasn't anyone near us. "I wasn't laughing at you, mate."

"I'm not your mate."

"Right," said Henry. "Not our mate. Don't even know each other." Henry tugged my arm and pulled me away. "Let's go this way, why don't we?" He turned away and I went with him, my back tingling, but it was Henry he kicked first and I swear I heard something break.

I wanted to check Henry but Wickes was turning toward me and I already knew how fast the bugger was. I blocked and blocked but his kicks were very strong and they hurt my arms or crashed through, anyway, only partially absorbed by my blocks. I tagged him once, good, with a front thrust kick that pushed him back clutching his side.

"Well, that's better than you did in the match," he said. His grin got nasty. "Guess I won't hold—"

I stepped back into *zenkutsudachi* and executed a *gedan-barai,* a low block.

He laughed at me. I was still ten feet away, but he began to lift his hands as I stepped forward and punched, face high.

I jumped the interval and my fist smashed into his mouth. He flew back and didn't get up.

Henry was sitting up clutching his side, his eyes wide. I checked Wickes—he had a pulse, he was breathing, he was bleeding from the mouth, and his eyes were blinking. I pinched his thigh, hard, and he yelped. "Feel that, do you? That's good enough for me." I went back to Henry and helped him up. "You okay, mate?"

"No. I think he broke a rib. And maybe I'm concussed."

I looked at him. "Why do you think that?"

"I blacked out there for a moment, when you hit him. I think. Saw it start, saw it finish—"

"What's my name? What's the date? Who's the prime minister?"

"Griff. It's Saturday the eighteenth. Tony Sodding Blair."

"Well, maybe you blinked. Should we find a bobby for Mr. Wickes?"

Henry surveyed the spreading blood on Wickes's chin. "No. I think he's got his."

I supported him back to the hotel and found Dr. Kolnick. The doctor was one of the senior members of the dojo, a third-degree black belt. I think his specialty was cardiology, but he'd spent so much time in the martial arts that he was good for the odd sprain and contusion.

Dr. Kolnick clucked his tongue and took Henry off to City Hospital and had him X-rayed, "to make sure we don't have a broken rib about to poke you in the lung." When the diagnosis turned out to be a hairline crack, he taped Henry up good. He also disinfected my hand. I had a gash below the knuckles I hadn't even noticed.

"Teeth, probably," the doctor said.

Teeth.

We caught our train back in the morning. Henry was stiff and I was sympathetic and tired and pissed off. "I don't think we should've turned our backs to him."

"Sod off," said Henry.

It felt weird, that trip. Except for the punch (and what a punch it was!) I didn't jump once. I arrived in Birmingham by train, walked around, and took the train back to London.

It felt . . . weird. It felt . . . normal.

Maybe normal was what I needed. Maybe I just needed to be in one place, where I only moved around like other people. Hmph. I could just see trying to rent a place. *How old are you, kid? Where's your parents? Tell me another.*

There was a fuss from Henry's parents about the cracked rib but they and Henry's headmaster ended up with the impression it had happened at the tournament itself and, as Henry said, "Better all around, that."

Sensei Patel wanted to talk to my parents about the fight, as he'd gotten specifics from us. I ended up bringing in a note, ostensibly from my dad, that "Griff discussed the whole thing with us and I appreciate the example you're setting for him. I am concerned about the incident, but believe it far less serious than what football hooligans are doing nowadays. And Griff has learned something from it."

I typed it on a rent-a-computer at Kinko's in San Diego and signed it left-handed, like the previous forms.

Sensei Patel said, "What'd you learn?"

"Don't turn my back."

"Kids!" But he didn't correct me. He did wonder aloud why my dad never came to classes or to watch any of the tests like the other parents.

"He's busy. Really busy."

In December, Henry went away, off to Amman for the holidays, and the dojo closed the week between. It was cold that year in London, I mean actual snow and stuff, so I went south, to the remote Bahía Chacacual. I took Consuelo and Sam with me, and with the dinghy sailed them west, away from La Crucecita, to the fishing village of St. Augustin. It was still only nine miles from the family compound as the crow flies, but thirty miles by road. There was a *colectivo* that ran inland to the Bahías de Huatulco International Airport and from there they could take the bus into town.

I was supposed to call for them in a week, the same place, weather permitting. That was the plan.

I put back out to sea and sailed east, hugging the coast, past Chacacual, past the little fishing village at Bahía Maguey, and after studying the shoreline carefully with my marine binoculars, on into Santa Cruz Bay with the sunset. There were dozens of dinghies, rigid and inflatable, tied up at the public pier. I stepped my mast before threading my way through them and tying up beneath the pier, where the posts weren't bumpered, but handy to ladder. I tied up and took the binoculars with me.

I wanted to see Alejandra.

It took me an hour to walk back into the hills above La Crucecita proper. I could've done it in thirty minutes if I hadn't been avoiding people and cars, but too many here knew my face.

I'd changed a bit. It was almost three years since I'd left and I was taller. I wore a baseball hat and a light jacket with the collar pulled up. It was windy and cool enough to justify the jacket. The offshore wind had been good for sailing—flat water, stiff breeze—but now it shook the trees and made it easy to imagine every sound an enemy.

The compound was lit up for a fiesta, a fire at the open end of the courtyard and lights strung across. I could hear music and the food smelled fantastic.

My stomach rumbled. *I'd even eat* chapulines *about now.*

I moved closer, working down through the brush; then, when the building blocked the way, I moved up into an old ahuehuete tree, using its thick trunk to shield my body, until I had a good view of the courtyard with the binocs.

There was Consuelo and Sam and her mother, Señora Monjarraz y Romera, and Alejandra's mother, Señora Monjarraz y Losada. Then I saw Rodrigo and a girl I remembered him chasing a few summers before, and then Alejandra came out of the house with a tray of food, with her cousin Marianna carrying another.

I stopped breathing for a moment. Alejandra was as beautiful as ever.

And she was okay.

I'd had reports, through Consuelo, but something inside of me must've still doubted, for I nearly choked on a sob. I blinked hard for a minute, then I could see properly again.

More cars and people made their way up the winding dirt road and the party expanded as the extended family and friends kept arriving. Most I recognized, though I would've been hard-pressed to come up with names, but there was a man who arrived with take-out from Sabor de Huatulco—I recognized the bag even if I didn't know him.

Rodrigo greeted him like some long-lost relative and I thought perhaps that's what he was, but then Rodrigo took him over and introduced him to Sam and Consuelo. I saw Sam's eyes narrow even though he smiled and shook hands, and while Consuelo looked polite, I'd seen her greet total strangers with more warmth.

I'd lay odds this was the new bellman from the Hotel Villa Blanca—the one who'd watched Alejandra's house while she was away.

I wanted to punch him, like I punched Wickes in Birmingham. Or jump him to the Isla la Montosa. Or that field with the bull in Oxfordshire.

Fat lot of good that would do.

Even if I killed him it would just draw them here in force,

maybe snatching Alejandra or Sam or Consuelo. Or all of them.

A piece of bark came off the branch where I'd been gripping it and I nearly fell out of the tree, nearly dropped the binocs.

I walked back into Santa Cruz and risked buying a meal at one of the tourist places, only speaking English. By the time I was finished, a three-quarter moon was rising, giving me enough light to sail back to Bahía Chacacual, though it was after midnight by the time I got there and jumped the dinghy back to the Hole.

They weren't back in St. Augustin the next week so I found a public phone and called the family compound, as arranged, and asked for Señora Consuelo. She was a while coming and I felt like something terrible must've happened but then she was there.

"¿Bueno?"

"Hola, Tía. ¿Quieres tomar el sol en la playa mañana?"

I didn't know if they were listening. Consuelo had several nephews so calling her aunt might throw them off. It would at least leave it in doubt. And she liked to sunbathe on the beach, or at least walk up and down the shore with the water washing over her ankles.

"No puedo ir. Volamos a casa mañana." So, they were being watched. The bastards might have checked the flight manifests into Huatulco and not found Sam and Consuelo.

Anyway, they were going to fly home and not risk meeting up with me again. Not in Oaxaca.

"*Que lástima. Vaya con Dios.*"

"*Debes tener cuidado.*"

"*Usted también.*"

Yeah, we'd all have to be careful.

Henry came back from the hols and brought me a little wooden horse, rearing, six inches high. "Merry Christmas and all that. It's olive wood. Didn't really know what you'd want."

I was touched but of course I couldn't show it. "Thanks. Didn't have to. I've got something for you, but it's back in me Hole. Bring it to class Thursday." I went to class most days, but for Henry it was Tuesday, Thursday, and odd Saturdays.

I didn't really have something for him. I'd bought something for Sam and Consuelo, and for Alejandra (mailed by Consuelo), but the season depressed me and I'd avoided the shopping crowds, the decorations, and the songs.

In Thailand, mostly.

In Phuket I was doing the same thing I did in Huatulco— I'd picked a remote jump site, in this case a little island called Ko Bon off Rawai. A resort on Phuket proper considered it their "private" island but I'd arrive on the south end, away from their *salas* and loungers and the honeymoon suite (though I watched some skinny-dipping once) and put my dinghy in the water and sail a half hour over to Chalong, avoiding the resorts.

I brought Henry a Thai Buddha head carved from rain-tree wood, gold leaf on the headdress thingy, pendulous earlobes and slitted eyes over a smiling mouth. It was the smile that made me buy it. Unlike the others, it was practically jolly.

He blinked when he opened it. "Very cool. How'd you know?"

"Know what?"

"I've got a shrine in my room. I'm not really Buddhist, but it's how I get out of Sunday chapel."

"You bleeding hypocrite!" I laughed.

He shrugged and smiled. "Yeah, well, you haven't had to listen to those bloody sermons on those bloody benches, have you? I'm all bony."

I shook my head. We were having our regular cuppa after but instead of walking, we were sticking to a corner table at the Expresso Bar. It was sleeting outside.

He opened his backpack to wedge the Buddha down inside with his *gi*. He pulled out a book to make room and I flipped through it. "Ugh. Exponents and polynomials. That was an ugly two weeks. Nearly ate me head."

"*Was?* Are you past this? I'm in advanced math, my form!"

"Uh. Did that last year. I'm homeschooled, you know? Work at me own pace. Do okay with the math." I reached up to touch his hair, a foot above me. "Over your head?"

"Oh, very funny." He licked his lips. "Give a guy a hand,

could you? I was supposed to work on it over the hols and I spent all my spare time, uh . . ." He blushed.

I sat up. "Oh, this has got to be good. Let's guess—there's a girl involved."

He punched my arm. "Well, it wasn't a boy, that's for sure."

"Jordanian?"

"Nah. Tricia Peterson—known her for years. Her mother is the protocol officer at the embassy, longtime friend of my parents."

"So you didn't do the math because you were snogging in the bushes."

He blushed redder. "Going around to see the sights. She doesn't live there, either. Visiting for the hols. Her school is out in the wilds of Oxfordshire. Girls' hell, she says."

I nodded. He had a girlfriend. I was thinking about Alejandra and I could sympathize and even be a little jealous.

"Show me what you're having trouble with. And I don't mean the snogging bit."

We did simplification of fractions with exponents until he had to run for the Tube. "Don't slip," I said. "It's like glass out there."

"Thanks for the help. Maybe you could help me again Saturday? I could ask for extra leave. We could do it at your place."

"That's a thought," I said, stalling. "Take us forever to get out there, though. Can you have guests in at your school? Never seen a boarding school—not outside a movie."

He looked at me like I was crazy. "Well, if that's your idea of fun. Sure. We'll go back there."

"Right."

I took a westbound train and transferred to a southbound at Earl's Court. Somewhere between Southfield and Wimbledon Park I jumped away to the Hole.

It snowed again, Friday night, very odd for London. Walking to the Tube station after class, Henry said, "'When men were all asleep the snow came flying, in large white flakes falling on the city brown.'"

I looked at him blankly.

"Robert Bridges. 'London Snow.'" He kicked at the snow on the sidewalk. "You know . . . poetry?"

"Ah. Me, I'm more of an 'As I was going to St. Ives' kind of guy. The bloody over the beautiful. Though I'm quite fond of Coleridge. And Green Day."

"But look at the *snow*!"

I scooped up a handful. "*You* look at it," I said, and flung it in his face. Much icy cold violence ensued and we had to shake the snow out of our clothes and hair while we waited on the platform.

St. Bartholomew's Academy is in an old Georgian mansion south of Russell Square. "But, of course, since *Prisoner of Azkaban* came out, we call it St Brutus's."

I looked at him blankly. The book had only just come out.

Henry explained. "His uncle pretends that Harry attends St. Brutus's Secure Centre for Incurably Criminal Boys."

I laughed. "Ah. Very good. Only read the first one so far."

"You could go *blind*! Look, I'll lend you two and three, okay?"

I nodded. I had odd feelings about it. Harry was an orphan, after all, whose parents were killed by someone out to kill Harry. A little too close to home, that.

We had to sign in with the school porter, a friendly man in a cardigan, in a room off the main hall.

The interior of St. Bart's was all polished wood and fusty old portraits staring disapprovingly at everyone. The students' rooms were somewhat better and you were more likely to see Manchester United or band posters instead.

Henry took me around to the dining hall and pulled some fruit ("All healthy snacks here—enough to make you croak") from the kitchen, then introduced me to a few people on his floor: "Griff, here, in my karate class. Helping me with my algebra."

His roommate, being a weekday boarder, was off with his folks in Ipswich, so we sat in there, the door open. I got to see his shrine, a shelf with a cotton meditation cushion before it, and some souvenirs from all over the world.

We did an hour of polynomials, then took a break. He showed me the gym in the basement, complete with boxing ring and some gymnastic equipment and balls and rackets and cricket bats. "Weather allowing, we use the green over at Brunswick Square for football and cricket. And the phys ed teacher's a right bastard about running. In any weather."

We did another half hour of math, then he lent me his

copies of *Chamber of Secrets* and *Prisoner,* and saw me down. On the stairs, he got asked, "Who's your girlfriend, 'enry?" by a large youth sitting on the landing with two others, all older than Henry.

Henry kept walking, his face still. When we were down in the main hallway and out of earshot he said, "That bastard is the reason I started karate."

"You turned your back on him."

"But you didn't. I noticed." Henry tilted his head. "Watters is the kind who'd go for your back, too, but not in front of witnesses. Last time he gave it a go I bloodied his nose. I got in trouble but so did he. He does petty things like pinching one's classwork or putting porn in your room and reporting it."

"That's why you locked your room."

"Yeah, had to start last year. Honor among gentlemen, my arse."

"Your parents know?"

"My dad went to this school. In his time, the odd bit of involuntary sodomy happened, so he thinks this is all just good, character-building experience. I mean, no danger of hemorrhoids, after all." Henry saw my face. "Hey, it's not that bad. My roommate's quite decent though his math is worse than mine, if you can imagine."

I shook my head. "I'll never bad-mouth homeschooling again."

I spent Sunday at Hogwarts. Well, reading on the beach in Oaxaca, really, but the books were good. I tried to get together with Sam and Consuelo but the code phrase *"No la conozco"* let me know they still thought they were being watched.

So I read. I'd finished both books by Monday night, so, having neglected my own schoolwork, I did an essay comparing the evolution of the magic use in all three books, in French. That's what I do when I miss Mum the most. Work in French.

I gave Henry a printout of the essay when I returned the books to him at Tuesday class. "Well, you're right about my vocabulary. Have to hit the *Dictionnaire Français-Anglais* for this one. Probably be good for me. Yuck." But he folded it carefully and tucked it into *Prisoner* before packing the books away in his bag.

We did the cuppa after and he said, "You know, I've got February half-term holiday coming up. Going to camp at my cousin's in Normandy. Think you could talk your folks into letting you go with me?"

I stalled. "Normandy? Where? Cherbourg?"

He shook his head. "Nah. Little village called Pontorson—less than ten kilometers from Mont-Saint-Michel."

I'd seen pictures of Mont-Saint-Michel. Who hasn't?

"Pretty. How do you go?"

"Train to Portsmouth. Night ferry to Saint-Malo. Cousin meets me at the ferry in his Citroën and takes me back to his cottage."

"There's no problem because of your age? Traveling, I mean?"

"Ah, there's more of a hassle coming home, so my cousin

usually crosses back and gets me through passport control, does a bit of shopping, and then heads back."

"What's he do, your cousin?"

"Retired—really my grandmother's cousin, what, mine twice removed? Something like that. He likes his wine. Likes to garden. Was a civil servant before. Transport, I think."

"Sure he'd be all right with it?"

"Oh, yeah. Suggested it before. Not you specifically— bring a chum, he said. He pretty much turns me loose when I'm there. I mean, if there's any heavy work in the garden, I pitch in, but there's woods and a river and there's a ten-minute bus you can take to the coast—the tide comes in like thunder, just miles of sand and then, *whoosh,* in it comes."

"Well, it sounds brilliant. Tell you what, I'll run it past *ma mère et mon père* and see what comes of it."

"I can have my mum call, if it'll help."

"Noted," I said. "If needed."

I should've said no.

EIGHT

Incursions

The smell woke me up, carrion-rotten, retch inducing. I followed it back through the cave toward the battery rack, a faint breeze in my face.

Something odd about that, since the airflow was usually the other direction—through the rubble that closed my little branch and up. It's two things—the water brings a bit of air in but also a network of cracks near the spring. The other thing is that the sun heats the rock around the upper end of the shaft, sucking up air from below.

But today, something else was happening and it really stank.

It had been so long since I'd been at the mouth of the mine that I couldn't remember it well enough to jump there. I finally had to jump to the pit toilet at the picnic area where I dumped my bucket toilet. It was overcast and surprisingly cold, unusual for here. That explained the airflow issue. The cold air was flowing down into the shaft. I jumped back for a jacket before I started the three-mile hike from the picnic area to the mineshaft.

When I got there I found the gate in the grate was wide open, the lock missing, the hasp mangled and streaked with copper. I looked at one of the depressions and realized someone had shot the lock off—the metallic streaks were from copper-jacketed bullets.

But the stench was up here, too.

I thought they were dogs, but realized after a moment that they were coyotes. Someone had shot them, shot the lock off the grate, and dumped them down.

It was illegal to hunt in the park, I was pretty sure. Even if a ranger had killed a coyote for some reason—rabies control, maybe—he wouldn't have shot the lock off and dumped them in the shaft.

Bastards.

I still had some rubber gloves from doing the concrete work in the Hole, but I jumped to San Diego and visited Home Depot for a paint-and-pesticide respirator mask and some heavy-duty plastic bags. The three coyotes were rotten with maggots and fell apart as I shoved them into the bags. They'd probably been there for days, but the change in the weather brought the smell in. Don't know how I could of stood it without the mask.

I left a note under the door at the rangers station telling them about the lock. It was after seven by then and the park had officially closed. It was better, as far as I was concerned, that the note be anonymous. If I started talking to the rangers, they might start wondering where I lived. The park had a residential ranger, but his quarters were way over by the park entrance, a good ten miles away.

I dumped the bags in their Dumpster.

There was a water spigot outside the station and I'd rinsed the gloves and was wiping them on a bit of turf near the station, preparatory to jumping back to the Hole, when I heard a gunshot.

It wasn't near—I didn't jump away or anything—but it did come from up the ridge, back toward the mine.

I jumped back up to the shaft, where I felt cold and exposed. The sun was going down and the wind was picking up. I walked back to one of the old surface buildings, a roofless rock-and-mortar shell, one wall tumbled down into a pile of its component rocks, and sheltered from the wind.

After a while, I heard another shot, loud, but still not so loud that it made me nervous. A motor started up in the distance, and then another.

Sounded like motorbikes. I started to leave the old building, trying for a vantage point where I might see them, when I realized the sound was getting louder.

They weren't motorbikes—they were four-wheeled ATVs, camouflage painted, two of them. They roared up the canyon scattering rock and dirt and what little grass there was and I wondered why I hadn't seen their tracks before. They each had another coyote on the back rack and telescopic rifles on a rack in front.

The gloves in my hand were still wet from washing, pretty clean, but the smell or the memory of the smell was still in my nose.

They pulled right up to the grate, flipped open the gate, and tossed them down. Just like that, not even looking around.

"Miller time!" one said to the other.

"Miller time," the other agreed.

I thought about tossing them down the shaft, but they hopped back on the ATVs and roared back down the canyon. Off-road vehicles were also illegal in the park.

I jumped back to the Hole and took the binoculars from the dinghy gear. I jumped to the ridgetop above the canyon, using the binoculars to pick my destination. They were easy to spot—they were in the long shadows of the Fish Creek Mountains and they'd turned their headlights on. I had to move once, as they moved behind a ridge, farther down the hills, but I tracked them all the way to the park's edge, to a light that showed through the gathering dusk.

I jumped back to the Dumpster by the rangers station and retrieved the plastic bags full of rotting coyote and left them, for the time being, in the old stone building I'd sheltered in, near the mineshaft.

I said yes to Henry about the trip to France. That is, I said it was all right with my parents.

"Do they need to talk to Harold? Or my mum?"

I shook my head. "They're cool. Tell you the truth, I suspect they can't be arsed."

He got this look on his face, like maybe he should be sympathetic, but then said, "Be a relief, that. Every permission thing I have to do involves faxes and international phone calls and crossing my *t*'s and dotting all the *i*'s. Your passport all in order?"

I nodded. "Oh, yeah. Old picture—hate it—but it doesn't expire for another three years."

"Right. I'll arrange the tickets."

"How much do you need?"

"Oh, no, Dad's treat. Thinks it's good I've got a friend outside of St. Brutus's. But I also think he wants cousin Harold to vet you since they can't themselves, not until summer."

"Oh, they coming home?"

"July after summer term. Three weeks. You going anywhere?"

"Too far in the future, mate. Anyway, I don't really pay

153

much attention to term holidays, what with the homeschooling. Better to travel when everyone isn't." Or so I heard.

In daylight, I used the binoculars and jumped, ridge to ridge, out to the edge of the park. There was a barbwire fence—not the park's—stretching along the boundary.

There were coyote carcasses, some old, some fresh, hung every thirty feet along the wire. Some of them were tatters of skin caught on the barbs and bones below.

On the other side of the fence, the ground was stripped bare, no vegetation, nothing, but there were sheep. Lots of sheep.

I moved down the fence, to the north, the direction the ATVs had seemed to go the night before. The fence turned a corner and there was a stretch of land that looked just like the park—it hadn't been grazed to nothing, but there were tire tracks—the kind with deep pockets from the tire lugs, designed to grip in mud and sand. I turned and followed them.

They went as far as a county road, dirt but graded smooth, then headed south, back along another fence. The coyote carcasses continued all around the property. The house was set back from the road, the only spot of vegetation on the entire ranch.

A mailbox at the road had "Keyhoe" painted crudely across it. The ATVs were parked near an outbuilding and there were four dogs lying on the porch that came for me, tearing across the ground toward the fence, growling and barking.

These were not friendly dogs.

I stepped off the road on the other side, put a mesquite bush between the house and me, and jumped away.

I took a cab into La Crucecita from St. Augustin. I was wearing tourist clothes and a big droopy sun hat. I gave directions in English and when the driver overcharged me, I didn't correct him. I went into Significado Claro like any other client. Alejandra was on the phone and I didn't look at her as she talked—I looked at the posters on the wall.

She glanced at my clothes and said, in English, "I'll be with you in a moment." I waved my hand, acknowledging this.

She was arranging the details for one of her immersion courses out at the Sheraton resort and I listened, not really paying attention to what she said, but just hungry for her voice.

Finally, details arranged, she hung up the phone and said, "How may I help you?"

I took off the hat and held my finger to my lips. They might be bugging the office.

Her eyes widened and without saying anything, she came around the desk and enfolded me in her arms.

I began crying.

"Shhhhh." Her arms tightened and I cried harder; after a while, I calmed down and she let go. I picked up a pad of paper and wrote on it, *¿Dónde podemos hablar?*

She took the pad and wrote where and when.

A half hour later we met on the wooded hillside behind the church, screened by the trees and with a good view of the approaches.

"No one was with me when I went into the church. I said ten Ave Marias," she told me and held up a bag, "and I brought *chapulines*."

She was kidding about the grasshoppers.

"I don't know what came over me," I said, over the chicken *enmoladas*. I'm okay, really."

"I missed you, too," Alejandra said.

I had to busy myself with eating for a moment, though I nearly choked. She covered by telling the news, new babies, two marriages, what was happening at the agency. I'd gotten some of this from Consuelo but I didn't tell her that. I just listened and watched. After a bit, when I'd finished eating, she said, "You look so muscular! Exercising?"

"Yeah, karate."

"And your schoolwork?"

"Yes, Mum. Every day."

She tilted her head. "Your English has changed—the accent, it's less American."

"Yeah, I've been mucking about in London."

"Don't tell me where," she cautioned.

"It's a big town, London—twelve million souls. But I don't live there."

"Et votre français?"

We switched to French.

"I still do written class work. I'm going to Normandy next month. Work on my accent."

"I'm jealous! I've been to Quebec and their French is . . . different. But Martinique in the French West Indies was good. But never to France."

"After next week, I can take you instantly."

She looked sorely tempted. "No. Maybe someday, when our friend from the Villa Blanca is gone, when they've stopped looking for you. Last time I went out of town, to Mexico City, they were there, watching to see who I met."

I could feel my face change, set.

"Don't feel bad. I do everything I would do otherwise, except see you. I just ignore them."

"Consuelo said they searched the house."

I saw anger flicker across her face but then she smiled. "But they didn't *take* anything. See? Not like a thief."

"They steal your privacy."

She shrugged and touched her forehead. "*This* is still private." She gestured between us. "*This* is still private."

She rolled up the paper trash from the lunch, twisting it tighter and tighter, then put it in my hand. "*You* can dispose of this. I will go back into the church and pray. How do you leave?"

I sighed. "I'll take the bus to Oaxaca, but I won't arrive. Twenty kilometers should be safe." I pulled the hat back over my eyes. "See? *Invisible*."

"We can meet here sometimes. Have Consuelo call the

157

day before—exactly twenty-four hours before—and she can say *el gato saliseo*. I will meet you the next day."

"Well, if the cat got out, the coyotes would eat it. Very well, if it is *safe,*" I added a little stridently.

She pulled me to her again. "If it is safe."

The dogs were nowhere to be seen when I appeared behind the bush on the other side of the county road from the ranch house. It was dark but the moon was three-quarters full and my eyes were acclimated. I jumped up to the porch, ripped the bags open, and dumped the rotting coyote corpses in front of the door.

The dogs began barking up a storm but I was back behind the bush before the first light came on.

"Oh, shit! Tasha, Linus, Jack, Lucy, get *out* of that!" I heard a thud and a dog's yelp. "Trey, get your rifle! Someone's messing with us!" I recognized the voice from when they'd dumped the last coyote.

I left before they started shooting randomly into the night. I hoped *all* of the dogs rolled in it.

"Why am I doing this?"

Henry reached out and adjusted my bow tie. It was a rented white-jacket dinner suit from a formal hire shop in Lewisham. They made me leave a bloody great deposit since I didn't have a credit card.

"Meet girls, have fun. Meet Tricia."

He'd only asked me two days in advance. I guess if your school is in a Georgian mansion and they have an honest-to-God ballroom, you occasionally have an honest-to-God ball. The St. Bartholomew's Midwinter Ball, to be specific.

"I went once before, when I first started at St. Brutus's, but spent the whole time against the wall. But Tricia's got leave to attend with her roommate and the girls from St. Margaret's come. It'll be fun."

We were waiting for Tricia at Paddington Station by the bronze statue of Isambard Kingdom Brunel. My hair was sticking up in back. I could feel it. I kept trying to push it down but Henry said, "Leave it alone. People will think you have nits."

"Git."

"Twit."

The 5:29 rolled in and Henry turned to watch. If he'd been my height, he would've been craning his neck and standing on tiptoe, but he didn't have to.

I'd realized early on that I was there for moral support. *What the hell—why not?*

Tricia really was stunning—tall, blond, green-eyed, and if she had any of Henry's problem with pimples, makeup was hiding it entirely. Her roommate was shorter, thank God, probably my height without heels, but slightly taller with. She had dark glossy hair half over her face, brown eyes, a turned-up nose.

"Griffin O'Conner, Martha Petersham."

"Delighted," she said.

"Charmed," I said, sounding rehearsed and phony and stupid.

We took the Tube back to Russell Square but a cab from the station, fog and drizzle not mixing well with rented clothing.

Tricia and Martha checked in with the headmaster as required and he placed the reassuring call back to St. Margaret's. They were to call again when they reached Martha's aunt's flat in Kensington Gardens after the ball.

Henry and I escorted them into the ballroom.

I don't know what I was expecting—probably something like a Merchant-Ivory production with a butler announcing the arrivals. It was kids in good clothes dancing to a nice punk band from the East End. Every six songs or so, the band would break and they'd play slow recorded music and a few students but mostly the chaperones would get out and fox-trot.

"I don't know how to dance," I told Martha early on, "but I'll take instruction."

This, apparently, was the right thing to say. I just thought about it like kata, or two-step *kumite,* and took instruction. She relaxed a great deal and bossed me around unmercifully. There was lots of laughter and some teasing because Henry and Tricia did all the slow dances.

Henry and I were returning from the refreshments table with drinks when we saw Watters, Henry's in-school nemesis, trying to pull Tricia onto the dance floor. I took one look at Henry's face and said loudly, "Why's the headmaster coming over here?"

Watters released her arm like he'd been scalded and turned.

Henry looked like *murder* so I stepped forward, between him and Watters, my drinks held out before me. "Watch out, drinks coming through!" I weaved a bit wildly and Watters stepped back, eyeing the drinks and still looking around for the headmaster.

Tricia, also eyeing Henry's expression, moved suddenly, taking Henry by the hand and saying, "I *love* this song." She pulled him onto the dance floor and kept moving until she was on the other side, near where two of the chaperones sat, nibbling cake.

I turned, more cautiously, and handed Martha her fizzy water. "Here you go, m'dear." I turned back to Watters and offered him the other. "Thirsty, mate?"

His reply was inarticulate. He turned on his heel and left. I didn't turn my back until he was well away so I was surprised when Martha kissed me on the cheek. I felt my ears go hot.

"What's that for?"

"Being clever," she said. "Being brilliant when it was needed." She was blushing a little, too. "Come on, dance."

We took a taxi after and Henry and I saw them all the way to the aunt's flat in Kensington Gardens.

Henry and Tricia snogged the whole way, and on the steps, before Martha punched the buzzer, I got kissed, too. And not on the cheek.

They scanned our passports, and along with fifteen hundred other souls, we trooped aboard the *MV Bretagne*. The brochure said it could handle over two thousand, but it was off-season. The cars had been loading for over an hour.

"Dad actually sprung for a cabin. Usually I just do the trip in one of the reclining chairs, which is a lot cheaper, but I guess there's a certain economy with two. He's not paying for two cabins, after all."

I nodded. I vaguely remember taking the ferry to Calais from Dover as a child and my mother insisting we not speak a word of English until we were back in the UK. I think they were both in graduate school then and we had three weeks off.

She was pretty serious about it and I learned the words for my favorite foods pretty quickly. *Pommes frites, Maman, s'il te plaît?*

They had a cinema aboard, bars, shops, several restaurants. We could've eaten in the fancier table service, Les Abers, but we hit the self-service place, La Baule, instead.

"Not fish and chips again?"

"Eat what you want."

I had the baguette with Brie and tomato and basil, and pie à la mode for pudding.

As we got out into the channel, the ship began pitching around and I began to regret the pie. We'd been thinking about hitting the cinema but it was something we'd both seen, so we returned to our tiny in-board cabin and lay down. Henry dropped off promptly but I couldn't get to sleep—it was still early afternoon by my clock. I started to get up again, but the ship was still dancing and my stomach lurched. I lay back down and dozed, more or less, through the night.

The ship was far calmer when we awoke, sheltered from the north winds by the Cotentin Peninsula. We got our stuff together, then hit the La Gerbe de Locronan café for tea and a roll. The Isle of Jersey was bathed in wisps of fog to the south. We docked at Saint-Malo at eight but it took a bit to get off.

Cousin Harold was waiting on the other side of passport control. "No trouble?"

"Not this time," said Henry. "Mr. Harold Langsford, young Master Griffin O'Conner."

We shook hands and I asked, "Is there trouble sometimes?"

Harold smiled. "Sometimes they get concerned about youngsters traveling alone. I've had to step up more than once to show he's being met. But," he looked up at Henry's face, "since Henry's shot up, I expect they're not paying that much attention." He glanced at the people streaming around us. "Let's give the car park a shot, why don't we? I'd like to clear out before they start unloading the cars."

It took less than forty-five minutes to make it to Pontsorson. We went on the coast road but it turned inland before we could see Mont-Saint-Michel. "Later," said Cousin Harold. "Don't want to go today, anyhow. There's less tourists during the week."

163

We had four days.

Cousin Harold's gray stone "cottage" had four bedrooms, a walled garden, and a vast slate roof. Everything in the garden was brown and wilted but tidy, beds well covered with mulch. It had been foggy in Portsmouth but by the time we parked his Citroën, the sun had burned off the light mist and the sky was blue as Mum's eyes.

Well, like they were.

His home wasn't quite in the village; it was fifteen minutes to walk in. "Thought we'd have lunch at the café." On the way he said, "You've just crossed into Normandy."

"It's not at the river?" The bridge was still ahead.

"No, in ancient times it was but now it's west of the river. There's a saying: 'The madness of the Couesnon put Mont-Saint-Michel in Normandy. But modern France doesn't depend on the vagaries of rivers."

He fed us fish soup and potatoes and salad and poured us half glasses of white Muscadet. "Right then, you bugger off—I'm going to take my nap. Tea at five?"

We walked around the village and Henry pointed out a large three-storied house with dormer windows sticking out of the slate roof and shielded by a wrought iron and stone wall. "That's haunted, you know."

"Tell me another."

"Well, doesn't it *look* like it's haunted?"

"Oh, aye. Movie-set haunted. Like the haunted house in Disneyland. They have that at Euro Disney?"

"They call it the Phantom Manor, I think."

We walked down around the Hotel Montgomery and then down by the river, the Couesnon, and the walkway that ran all the way to Mont-Saint-Michel.

The sun made everything lovely—still, warm air—and I took off my jacket and tied it around my waist. Back by the train station there were lots of little models of the Mont and I asked the clerk, a bored young woman, which she thought I should buy, to try my French. She looked at me like I was crazy but entered into a conversation readily enough. I began saying things like, "Well, if I wanted to hit someone, which would be the best? And which do you recommend for throwing? For feeding to disliked relatives? For clogging a toilet?"

This killed thirty minutes and I could feel my ear for the accent improving. She asked where we were from and, fortunately, didn't want to try her English when she found out. Then a large busload of tourists returned from the Mont and filled the shop, killing time before their train. I bought a medium brass Mont and a postcard and we fled from the crowd.

"Well, your accent is still atrocious," said Henry.

"*She* didn't seem to have any trouble understanding me."

"Triumph of content over style. Your vocabulary is still bigger. Couldn't follow all of it."

"Thought you studied it in school?"

"Used to. This year it's Arabic."

"Oh."

"Because it looks like my parents are making a speciality of the Middle East. And, er . . ."

165

"And?"

"Tricia, too. She's fluent."

I laughed and laughed, until he turned red and punched my arm.

"Nous devrions parler seulement français tandis que nous sommes ici."

He had me say it more slowly and finally got it.

So we did—only French for the rest of the trip. Cousin Harold was fine with it. He'd been fluent for years. Henry didn't talk near as much as he usually did but we worked hard to drag him into conversations.

The next day, Henry and I walked all the ten kilometers to the Mont and spent the day wandering from Gautier's Leap to Gabriel's Tower, then spent some time toddling around the mud banks, though we stayed away from the areas marked SABLES MOUVANTS!

I discussed it with Henry, in French of course. He picked up a rock and heaved it onto the wet sand and *bloop*, it sank right down. Very quick sand indeed.

I sketched a great deal, annoying Henry, who was snapping pics with his camera, but got a good sketch of the lace staircase and the statue of Saint Michael slaying the dragon. He kept wanting me to hurry up but I'd just send him off to get us drinks or snacks.

Having decided we'd walked quite enough, we took the train station shuttle back to Pontorson.

We relaxed the next day, helped Cousin Harold clear

leaves out of his roof gutters. I sketched, and we watched a Manchester United match on the telly. We were keeping the deal though, not speaking anything but French.

By the time the *MV Bretagne* had pulled into Portsmouth (Cousin Harold came back with us, to hand us through passport control and do some shopping) my accent was much better and we'd managed to increase Henry's vocabulary by about fifty words.

"You visit me this summer and we'll make a real breakthrough—get you speaking like Griff here," said Cousin Harold, finally reverting to English while we waited in the British-citizen line at immigration.

They were scanning the bar code on the passports and glancing at the pictures, and saying, "Welcome back, welcome back, welcome ba—" The terminal beeped when they scanned my passport and two bored-looking guards leaning against the wall were suddenly blocking the route out to the car park and the taxis and the buses.

"Mr. O'Conner, I'm afraid I'll need you to go with these officers."

Shit! "What's wrong?" I asked. "Did my passport expire?"

He shook his head. "No."

Cousin Harold and Henry had gone through before me and gotten yards on the way, but Henry tugged on Harold's elbow and they came back. "What seems to be the problem, Officer?"

"Are you traveling with this lad, sir?"

"Indeed I am. *In loco parentis,* so to speak. Were you worried he was an unaccompanied minor?"

"No, sir. There's an alert out. He's wanted for questioning."

"Questioning? For what? I should really call his parents, then."

"I'd be surprised if you could, sir. According to this alert, they were murdered six years ago. This lad's been missing ever since."

Henry was frowning but when he heard this his eyes went wide. "Nonsense. Griff's dad teaches computers and his mother teaches French lit."

The immigration control officer narrowed his eyes and looked interestedly at Henry. "Tell you that, did he?"

"Stop it," I said to Henry. "That's what they did, all right. Before—" My voice broke and I clamped my mouth shut.

Cousin Harold frowned at me. "Surely, Officer, you don't expect this boy to have anything to do with this crime?"

The officer shrugged. "It just says 'detain for questioning.' Until four days ago he was presumed dead." His phone rang and he picked it up. "Yes, sir. We've got him. *Your* office? Yes, sir." He hung up and spoke to the two guards. "The chief wants him." He handed my passport to one of them.

It was Henry's eyes that hurt. "They came for us in California," I said. "I got away but Mum and Dad—" I took another breath. "Anyway, that's the only thing I wasn't honest about, if you were wondering."

"Here, boy, let me take that for you," one of the guards

said, taking hold of my bag. The one with my passport took hold of my upper arm, firmly. Pretty much like the other guard had taken my suitcase.

"If you'd care to come this way, sir," he said to Cousin Harold.

Henry said, "Someone killed your parents? Who did that?"

I shook my head. "It's complicated."

They took us through a door with a punch-button combination lock, then down a hallway toward a bank of lifts. Ahead on the right was a double set of doors with the universal pictograms.

I pointed. "Need to use the loo. Urgently."

They looked at each other and the one holding me shrugged. "Right, then." He pushed the door open and said, "Take off your coat and turn out your pockets." Cousin Harold and Henry stayed in the hall with the other immigration officer.

"What?"

"Come on—you want to use the lav, do what I say."

I took the coat off—it was my favorite jacket, a leather one—and handed it to him. I put my wallet on the counter and a handful of French coins. "That's it. Why?"

"Routine. Don't want you doing yourself an injury. Show me your ankles."

I pulled up my pant legs. "No knives. No guns," I said. I gestured at my thin wallet and the coins. "All right?"

He nodded and pointed at a stall. "Help yourself."

The minute I locked the stall door behind me, I jumped.

It was a sloppy jump, unfocused, and pieces of porcelain and water splashed across my shoes and the limestone floor of my Hole. I hated to think what the stall looked like. Bet he heard it. I pictured his steps pounding—no, splashing—across the floor and his opening the door to see the shattered toilet, maybe toilet paper strewn everywhere.

And no me.

NINE

Shattered Tiles

So, it had to be the passport. They'd scanned it on my way to France. Someone had noticed and the alert was put in the system.

It could've been just the normal authorities. Surely the consular people had got involved when my parents were killed. After all, I'd gone missing. I should never have gone through customs. I should've jumped past, instead, or directly onto the boat in the night. On the way back, I shouldn't have even *used* the boat.

And now they'd watch Henry. They'd watch the health club where I took karate.

When will you learn, you git?

I moped around the Hole for a few days, then jumped back to London. I was ultra-careful, popping into the field in Oxfordshire and doing the rest by train. No jumping. It was the weather for coats, fortunately, freezing rain, and I wore a big anorak with the hood pulled well forward.

Henry came out of the health club after evening class and headed for the Knightsbridge station. His head was down and his shoulders were rounded. No after-class cuppa. I followed, distantly. There were several other people going down the street toward the station and I decided against going in. Cabs were scarce, because of the cold rain, but I lucked into one dropping a fare at Harrods and had him take me straight to Russell Square. Henry exited ten minutes after, as did several others. Two men in identical dark green overcoats followed him all the way back to St. Bartholomew's.

One of them was Kemp, the man from Bristol, the man who'd been there the night my parents died.

I nearly jumped on the spot.

Whoa, boy. You want to confirm that you're hangin' about?

I headed in the other direction, toward Holborn Station, and ten minutes later stepped onto an eastbound Central train and rode it all the way to the end of the line at Epping.

JUMPER: GRIFFIN'S STORY

I walked out into the car park shrouded in the rain and hesitated. No, if they could feel me jump sixteen miles away from Henry's school, I didn't care. Nothing to tie me to Henry, even if they could feel it.

And I was sick of the rain.

I basked on the beach in Phuket the next morning. I was chilled through—I thought it was the dampness of the cave, but even on the beach, in the hot sun, I felt cold. The water looked unappealing as a result but ultimately it was the cure.

It felt like a bath after the freezing rain in London. Not exactly hot, but certainly warm. Later I got breakfast from a street vendor, fresh pineapple and grilled garlic sausages and sticky rice, and ate it in the sticky shade of a mango tree.

At the Kinko's in San Diego, I wrote:

HEY, HENRY,

I'M SORRY YOU GOT CAUGHT UP IN MY STUFF. I DID LIE TO YOU ABOUT MY PARENTS BEING ALIVE BUT I HAD TO LIE TO THE DOJO, TOO. THE PEOPLE WHO KILLED THEM ARE STILL AFTER ME. I LOOK AT THIS AND IT SOUNDS RIDICULOUS, PARANOID AS HELL, BUT THAT DOESN'T MAKE IT ANY LESS TRUE. I STARTED TO VISIT YOU AND THEY WERE THERE, FOLLOWING YOU.

SO, IT'S BEEN REAL. KEEP ON TOP OF YOUR MATH. SAY GOOD-BYE FOR ME.

YOUR FRIEND,
GRIFFIN

I posted it from way the hell out in Buckinghamshire, at the Chesham post office. I had my doubts about it. If they saw it, I hoped they'd understand I wouldn't be seeing Henry again. If they didn't intercept it, I hoped he'd understand that—well, I just hoped he'd understand.

I'd almost said, "Say good-bye to Tricia and Martha." Then I'd amended it to, "Say good-bye to the girls." And I thought about Kemp and his lot watching them, following them.

As I said, I hoped Henry would understand.

Obviously, I stopped going to karate. And I laid off London completely for a while.

This didn't mean I stopped doing karate. I worked on my katas and I bought a dozen *makiwari,* practice boards you plant in the earth with padded striking surfaces covered in rope about shoulder high. I scattered them around the Empty Quarter, up and down the gully.

Now if I'd been doing regular strikes, I could've gotten along with just one target. You just stand in front of it and whack it, after all—punches, knife hand, elbow, and kicks— but I wasn't doing it like that.

I started the strikes while I was still yards away. It was like that time in Birmingham, when I punched Wickes, the tournament cheat. Begin the strike, jump, and connect.

Except when I didn't.

I scraped my shin and forearm, cut knuckles, and once I

bloodied my own nose. I'd jumped too close, clipped the board with my fist but shot past, and it sprang back full in my face.

I nearly gave it up right then, but I was back the next day, swollen nose and all.

I bought one of those solar showers, the plastic ones for camping, and hung it from the south side of an ahuehuete tree in the jungle behind Bahía Chacacual. Depending how much overcast there was, I'd shower sometime between midday and the afternoon. I tried not to leave it too late. If it was cloudless, it got too hot and I had to add cold water. I'd always jump it back to my Hole and refill it from the spring when I was done, then hang it back so it would be ready the next day.

Except for the odd rainy day, it worked out well, and if I was desperate, I'd wash in the rain. I didn't have to worry about memberships or people messing with me and I could see the bright Pacific through the trees. And you didn't want to linger, because the mosquitoes could be bad, especially at dusk.

I took a train from Saint-Malo, jumping to the car park at the ferry, changing some American cash to *monnaie français* in the terminal, then walking to the train station. Besides the cash and an oversized coat, all I carried was my sketchpad and some pencils, which was a damn good thing. The streets swarmed with tourists and I would've hated to be carrying a bag. As it was, I was hit several times by others' luggage.

Doing it like this, there were no customs agents, no passports scanned, no checkpoints. I was nervous about it, wondering if they'd posted anyone there. I thought Cousin Harold's place in Pontorson was more likely being watched, but I sat in the corner of a car and looked for familiar faces, green trench coats, anyone watching me, but the only persons who paid any attention were the conductor and my seat mates, an old French couple and a nervous Spaniard with no French or English.

Like me, he was going to Paris and was worried he was on the wrong train. While he talked funny (I thought) with his Castillian *gra-th-ias,* he had no trouble understanding me so immediately asked all sorts of questions to which I didn't know the answers. I spent the ride acting as a conduit between him and the elderly French couple, as they had the answers and were more than happy to tell him about his train transfer in Rennes and the best subway stop for his hotel in Paris. They showed pictures of their children and grandchildren. The Spaniard showed a picture of his parents and his sisters and his sisters' children. By the end of the hour trip into Rennes my throat was dry and my *español* was becoming *ethpañol.*

The couple said *au revoir* in Rennes and I helped my Spanish friend to his train. His transfer was imminent but my train didn't leave for two hours—the penalty of buying the tickets that day instead of reserving ahead. He thanked me effusively upon boarding. I waved and walked away feeling both relieved and sad.

I ate the *plat du jour* in a creperie in the next block over from the train station. After, I walked a bit and sketched. I boarded my train in good time, found the seat, and after having my ticket punched, slept the two hours into Paris.

The Gare Montparnasse was all glass and people, end-of-business-day crowds swarming to catch trains out of Paris. Still half asleep, I found a restroom and, very carefully, jumped home.

This time I didn't break the toilet.

It isn't hard to get fed in Paris if they think you're French, but it is amazing how hard it is to get served otherwise. My accent was apparently improving enough and, it seemed, kids were wearing similar enough clothes that I fit in.

I sketched a lot—the bridges over the Seine mostly, and interesting faces, if they were sitting still. One day, in a café, I began drawing a random head, no live subject in mind, and the outline of the head, particularly a sharp turn between the forehead and the top, felt familiar. I kept scribbling, faster, and faster, more an impressionist caricature than my usual style, but I captured it, that feeling of familiarity.

Only then did I realize it was Kemp, the Bristol-accented bastard who'd been there in San Diego, who'd been there in Oaxaca and London. I tore it out of the sketchbook, my hands spread to crumple it into a ball, but I stopped myself.

"C'est bon. Votre père?" The waiter, passing by, surprised me.

I was angry. The drawing didn't look anything like me!

"Non. Un homme mauvais." A very bad man. Definitely *not* my father.

The waiter shrugged. *"Mon père est un homme mauvais."* He moved on before I said anything.

Perhaps if my father had been a bad man, I wouldn't miss him so.

When I left, I carefully put the loose drawing in the back of my sketchbook.

I stole some plywood paneling from a construction site, six sheets, four feet by eight, and leaned them against the wall of the cave. There wasn't anyplace to pin up my drawings otherwise. The limestone was often damp and never flat, and my refrigerator, the little twelve-volt job, wasn't exactly magnet heaven. One drawing overwhelmed it. I put six plywood sheets up, five of them as edge to edge as the irregular surfaces allowed.

The one on the end, separated by a good yard, became the villains' gallery—as far from my bed as possible—and while the rest were lit with lamps that were part of the regular circuit, I put in a separate light and switch for that end panel.

I started with Kemp.

I tried others—the woman who'd been there the night my parents died. The man I'd shot in the eyes with the paintball gun. The man I'd shot in the bollocks and then hit several times with the gun. But even though I could remember the woman's voice, the visual memory wasn't there. I tried but it was like drawing made-up comic book characters—no real basis in reality.

The big guy, from Oaxaca, the one I'd scared over the cliff—him I managed. It was that surprised and panicky look as he flinched over the edge. I also managed Señor Ortiz from the Agencia Federal de Investigación, though I didn't really count him as one of *them*. More of a minion—support staff, if you will. And I drew a good head shot of Mateo the bellman as I'd seen him that night at the *fiesta de Navidad*.

They could feel it when I jumped. *They* were dangerous. *They* wanted me dead. Maybe Ortiz did, too, but he wasn't the same level of threat.

I put the big man and Mateo up with Kemp. Ortiz I put down below. I scribbled stuff on the edges: where, when, and who, if I knew it.

Later I added a biggish world map. I used little Post-its for "named" ones. Kemp got one in Oaxaca and San Diego and London. Ortiz, the big man, and Mateo got one in Oaxaca. Then I put two pins in London for the guys who'd found me in the subway. I couldn't remember them well enough to draw them. Three other pins went to San Diego for the woman and the other two men who'd been there with Kemp.

That made seven, not counting Ortiz. Yet they'd detected me in London, so at least one had been stationed there, or traveling through, but it made sense, if they had enough of 'em, to station a "Sensitive" in major cities.

I wrote "Sensitives" on a big scrap of drawing paper and

pinned it above the drawings of Kemp, the big man, and the bellman, Mateo. On another scrap I wrote, "Minions," and pinned it below, above Ortiz.

Then I went back to the library in San Diego and got printouts from the microfilm collection of the newspapers, the *News Daily* and the *Union Tribune*—the stories that told about that night, the murder of my parents.

On the side of the El Centro Ranch Market, there's this mural of women doing laundry in the river. One of them wears only her underwear—it's not exactly explicit but I still liked looking at it.

From the pay phone in the front of the store, I called Sam's number and, as usual, asked for Rosa in *español*. Sam's voice was hoarse and instead of using either of the code phrases ("*número incorrecto*" or "*No la conozco*") he said, "Griffin, I need you here now. They've got Consuelo."

I drew breath to say "Who?" and another voice came on the line.

"Come on, Griffin. Don't make me hurt 'em." That thick Bristol accent was unmistakable. How on earth did he keep it? Didn't Kemp ever watch BBC as a kid?

"Let them go," I said. "Leave them alone."

"Don't waste their time, boy." He hung up.

I took a step to the left and lashed out, kicking the trash barrel over violently; my foot came down in the Empty Quarter, sand and trash swirling around me. I felt like throwing up.

I jumped to the Texaco petrol station and used the phone there, starting with 911. "There are men with guns holding Sam Coulton at his ranch house. They're torturing him—they're trying to get his bank account access numbers from him. No, I won't give you my name."

I hung up. They'd know where the call came from, of course, but the petrol station was a long way from nowhere.

The next number I had to get out of the phone book. When they answered I spoke in Spanish. "There are coyotes with guns at the ranch of Sam Coulton. They have thirty illegals and are waiting for their transport to meet them. If you hurry—" I hung up, not even waiting for the questions. I jumped to the turnoff—the place on old Highway 80 where the county dirt road joined the asphalt—and began walking. It was over seven miles to the ranch house but I didn't want them to feel my arrival and, if my calls worked, I might be able to hitch a ride.

An INS helicopter roared out of the east, probably coming from El Centro. They came in low, maybe seventy feet, obviously following the highway, then banking hard at the turnoff. I thought for a moment they were doing that for navigation, but I realized they wanted to spot any fleeing vehicles. This was the only road out.

I crouched off the road, in the mesquite, when I heard them, well before they flashed by overhead. I shook my fist in the air.

Go, go, GO!

I started running but that didn't last. I was still over five miles away and it was hot and the sun was like a hammer. The road ducked up and down, over a set of low ridges, and I couldn't see or hear *anything*. Well, I heard *something*.

I got behind a stand of cholla before the sheriff's car came over the ridge behind me. It was followed almost immediately by an SUV in INS white and green and then an INS passenger van.

For my imaginary illegal aliens.

They bunched up and slowed, bumping through a washed-out section of the road on the way up the next ridge. I was out into the road and running, crouched low, trying to get behind the van before they noticed me in the rearview mirror.

I didn't have to worry—the patrol car, in the lead, should've brought up the rear. Three INS agents piled out of their SUV to push the patrol car past the point it was bottoming out.

I considered jumping into the interior of the van, but found I could crouch on the box receiver of its trailer hitch and hold on to the spare-tire rack. *Good.* Didn't want to jump—didn't want to clue in Kemp and his bunch.

Just let Sam and Consuelo be all right.

I dropped off the van while it bounced across a particularly nasty pothole and then rolled sideways into the brush. I got stuck by a prickly pear, hiding in a tuft of brown grass, but the van didn't stop, so I guess they didn't notice.

I scrambled through the brush, headed for the back of the stable.

The first thing I saw was one of the INS agents going by with an M-16 assault rifle. I ducked back into the brush. The second thing I saw was another INS agent.

He was dead. Very clearly dead. His head was half off and the blood was worse than—it was worse than *that* night. I gagged and moved carefully back into the bush, breathing through my nose, but finally, I couldn't help it—I vomited into the sand.

There was a big green SUV I didn't recognize—not Sam's and it certainly wasn't an official vehicle. It also hadn't passed me on the dirt road. Kemp's people must've come in it.

He's still here?

I came up behind the car from the county sheriff's department. There was an officer talking on the radio, but he wasn't seated. He was crouched on the ground, shielded by the open door. "—forensics for sure, and body bags—uh, two for the residents and there were six INS guys on the chopper—five agents and the pilot."

"Got that, Joe," the radio crackled. "We've got our chopper up and heading your way, eyes wide open. Hopefully they'll spot the missing chopper. Sheriff says secure the crime scene."

I couldn't help myself.

I jumped into the house.

Sam was on the rug before the couch, his hands bound behind him with a plastic cable tie. Consuelo lay in the doorway to the kitchen. The rug had soaked up most of Sam's blood but in the kitchen it spread across the linoleum as far as the refrigerator and the cabinet.

I stuffed my fist in my mouth to keep from screaming.

There were footsteps on the porch outside, perhaps the deputy or one of the INS agents returning after checking the outbuildings.

In the Empty Quarter I took my hand out of my mouth and screamed.

I jumped to La Crucecita, to Alejandra's office at Significado Claro, but she wasn't there. I stared at my watch, juggling time zones with difficulty. Lunch—right.

I jumped to her house. Not there, either. I looked out the window, toward the hotel.

Mateo, the bellman, was striding up the sidewalk, a shoulder bag dangling from his hand, as if he'd snatched it up. He talked to a cell phone in his other hand.

I jumped to the next window and saw him jerk his head around, looking at the house. He was definitely one of the Sensitives.

I started in the living room, two quick steps forward, and jumped into the air.

The sole of my foot smashed into Mateo's chest hard enough to send him flying backward, his feet coming up waist high before he crashed to the sidewalk. I saw his head bounce and his eyes rolled back.

I bent over to check his pulse and he swung at me, weakly.
I kicked him in the side, then grabbed him by his shirt and
jumped five miles east, to the beach on Isla la Montosa, and
spilled him half in sand, half in water. I pulled his wallet out.
He'd dropped the phone and the bag, so I went back for them,
before I returned to Alejandra's office.

She still wasn't there and I was very afraid that they'd
taken her already. I let myself out and started asking questions: *"¿Usted ha visto Alejandra?"*

She wasn't at any of her regular lunch places and no one
had seen her. There was a burning at the back of my nose
and I was having trouble seeing. *They've already got her.*
Then I saw her, coming across la Plaza Principal from the
direction of the church, and my knees nearly buckled with
the relief.

She took one look at me and her face went white. "What
is it?"

I jumped her to her house, without asking, without warning.

She dropped to the floor. "Now I *know* it is bad."

"You need to pack," I said. "Whatever you care about."

She blinked. "Tell me! What is it?"

"They killed Consuelo and Sam."

"¿Muertos? ¡No!" Both hands went to her face and her
breath started coming in short, convulsive gasps, then sobs.

And that broke me, too.

I dropped to my knees and wrapped my arms around her

185

and began sobbing as hard, then harder than her. Her arms pulled me in and I wrenched away. "No! They'll come! You need to pack."

She took one of the kitchen towels and blew her nose hard. "Where?" she managed after a moment.

I opened my mouth to speak and then blinked. "New York City," I said out loud, but then I shook my head vigorously and pointed at my ear and then around the room. She had an erasable whiteboard mounted on one of the cabinet doors. I grabbed the marker and wrote, "France," making sure she saw it, then took the dish towel she'd blown her nose with and wiped the writing off the board.

"What about him?" she said, pointing toward the Hotel Villa Blanca.

"Mateo? I took him on a trip. We've got some time, but I don't know how long." I had no idea if Mateo had local backup or not. How would they have taken me, anyway? I pushed her toward her room. "Pack, please!"

I'd stuffed Mateo's phone in my pocket and I took it out, curious. There were several programmed numbers but most of them were international. Two were local, though. One said "*Tio,*" meaning "uncle," and the other said "Detonar." Dee-toner? I was confused, then realized that *tio* was in Spanish, so I sounded it out. Day-Toe-Nar.

"*¿Alejandra, como se dice 'detonar' en inglés?*"

She looked up. "Detonate? Explode?"

Oh, shit.

I grabbed her and jumped. She staggered away from me in the Empty Quarter, dust and underwear swirling around us.

"What?" she yelled. She looked angry and frightened.

I held up the phone. "I took this from Mateo. Look." I stabbed my finger at the quick-dial entry: *Detonar.*

She read it and bit her lip. "We don't know what that refers to." She began scooping up her panties and bras. "It could be anything."

"And it could mean one very specific thing."

She shook her head in frustration. "*You* have the phone, though."

"It's just a phone. Who *else* has that number?"

"I want my things!"

I jumped us to the Hole and left the bag and her clothes on the table. She opened her mouth to ask but I said, "This is my place. It's an old mine. I *detonar* the entry so the only way in or out is my way."

"My things?"

I licked my lips. "Let's go see, okay?"

It took me a minute, but I eventually remembered the roof of the hotel well enough to jump. The memory wasn't from the last time I'd been there, sneaking up on Kemp, but from one of the firework-viewing parties.

I crouched at the parapet with Alejandra and looked over the patio and the swimming pool and the tennis courts to her house.

"See," she said. "You are too cautious."

I nearly broke down. "No. Not anywhere near cautious enough or Sam and Consuelo—"

She nearly lost it, too. "Okay!" She chopped down with her hand, cutting me off.

"What's your first priority?" I said, pointing toward the house. "What's the most important thing in there?"

"My mother's jewelry, up on the closet shelf. The rosewood box."

"And then?"

"The photo albums—you know, in the living room."

I took a deep breath and jumped to her room. The closet door was already open from before, and I stood on tiptoe and snagged the box. As it dropped into my hand, I jumped back.

"Here," I said, pushing the box into her hands. I pictured the living room and then we both flinched at the flash of light and the horribly loud, flat crack that shook us, and then the tile roof of her house rose up and scattered like confetti in smoke.

I jumped her and the box away as the first fragments began to fall around us.

TEN

Turning the Corner

killed them."

Alejandra had been crying for about a half hour, lying on my bed. I'd tried patting her back, but I couldn't keep still. I'd tried pacing, then I'd jumped away, to the *makiwara* in the Empty Quarter, and hit them, hit them, hit them until my

189

knuckles split, bleeding, and the pain was finally enough to cut through the other pain.

I was sitting by the cave pool, soaking my hand in the icy cold water, when I said it.

Alejandra, lying on her side, staring into the dark corner of the cave, lifted her head. "What?"

"I killed Sam and Consuelo."

I'd told her the circumstances already—the INS and the helicopter and the phone calls. The way I'd found them.

A look of understanding came over her face and that was more painful than anything.

"I killed them like I killed my parents. Like I killed that policeman in San Diego." My voice was ragged; my breathing cut through the cave like a coarse-tooth saw. "Okay, I didn't hold the knives, but I might as well have."

I looked at her and away. "And I've probably killed you."

"*¡Callete!*" she said. "Stop it."

I took another ragged breath and held it. She got up and came over. "*Hay caramba!* What did you do to your hand?" She took it out of the water. The bleeding had slowed. "Did you hit someone? Mateo?"

"Mateo? Oh, Christ!"

I jumped.

Mateo wasn't on the island. It was a fairly short swim to the mainland, or he could've flagged down one of the dive boats and gotten a ride. I'd kicked him pretty hard, though, and his head did bang against the sidewalk.

So maybe he drowned in the strait.

190

I resented it either way, because I really wanted to hit someone.

When I appeared back in the Hole, Alejandra said, "Never do that again!" Her voice was strident and I flinched.

"Do what?"

She gestured sharply around. "You said there's no exit. What do I do when they kill *you*?"

"I'm sorry," I said, but that phrase was like a can opener. "I'm sorry! Oh, God, I'm so sorry!"

She put me on the bed and held me while the sobs wracked me over and over again. Sometimes she cried, too; eventually we slept.

She stayed with me five days. With me—I never left her in the Hole if I wasn't there, even if it was just fetching food from Phuket or the West End. We'd take turns with the solar shower in the jungle near Bahía Chacacual, the other waiting down the hill (though I peeked once. Oh. My. I was uncomfortable for hours).

I'd sleep on my side, away from her, aware of her every motion.

On the sixth day, we shopped—Harrods in Knightsbridge—clothes and luggage. Back in the Hole we took the store tags off everything and packed them away in the two bags. I put fifty thousand dollars in the bottom of her main case without telling her. In London I'd already changed a thousand dollars to francs at Barclays.

"Don't flash it," I said.

"No, I'm not *too* stupid."

The corners of my mouth turned down and she laughed. *"¡Solo estaba bromeando!"* She pulled me to her and kissed my forehead, without bending. "Ai."

We jumped to Rennes and waited for *them* but apparently it wasn't the sort of place *they* were monitoring. I started to buy the ticket for her but she stopped me. "Sweet, but I must do for myself now, eh?"

The clerk delighted in helping her with the transaction and came out of his booth to direct her to the right platform for the Paris express. I bought a southbound ticket for Saint-Nazaire on the Bay of Biscay.

I had this picture of me standing on the platform, watching her train pull away, but I wasn't paying enough attention when I purchased my ticket—mine left first. She walked me to my platform, held me for a moment, hard, as if to take an impression with her flesh, an indented memory. Then she kissed me, on the mouth, a grown-up kiss that brought the blood rushing.

"Be careful—*sois prudent!*" And then she was walking away, her shoulder bag slung, her large suitcase trailing behind on its wheels.

I rode the train as far south as Redon and jumped away, from the space between the cars.

The papers said the helicopter was abandoned in Mexico, just over the border near Highway 2, the route to Tijuana.

There were no cars reported hijacked but there was also no sign of the fugitives.

Apparently the police theory was drugs. Drug smugglers killed the INS agents and Sam Coulton and Consuelo Monjarraz y Romera. And they fled back into Mexico.

Sam's funeral was in El Centro, Consuelo's in La Crucecita. I didn't go to either. What could result but more death?

And not the right victims.

I tried to jump to Phuket, not my usual place out on Ko Bon island, but an alley near the market in Chalong, but I couldn't recall it well enough.

I jumped my dinghy to the island instead and sailed over, and, when I got there, I spent fifteen minutes sketching the spot.

My plywood wall of sketches began having another purpose. If I wanted to return regularly to a place, I'd record it. Maybe photographs would've worked but when you sketch a place, you really *look* at it.

And I tried to sketch Mum. Then Dad.

Couldn't.

It wasn't memory—their faces were as clear as the day they—well, they were clear. But I couldn't see through the tears and my hands shook. It's hard to draw when your hands want to make fists.

It was the same with Sam and Consuelo, though I managed a head and shoulders portrait of Alejandra.

I tried another drawing of Mateo, as I'd last seen him, half in the water, half out, on the beach at Isla la Montosa. That I managed with some degree of accuracy.

I knew it was accurate—I had his driver's license. I also had his bag, which had held a gun—an odd gun.

I'd fired it in the desert, at a limestone outcropping, and it put two spikes into the stone with a cable taut between them. When I touched the cable it shocked the shit out of me, numbing my entire arm.

There were five more cartridges in the bag, all identical. The gun folded open at the breech, like an old-fashioned shotgun. I fired one more and it, too, shot out cable and two spikes. I didn't touch it this time. I put the bag back in my Hole.

I tried to relax, to do nothing, but when I did, I found myself wandering down to the end of the cave and turning on the flood that lit my villains' gallery. There were only four sketches. I thought there should be more.

I knew they were in London—they'd tried for me twice there, so I figured that was the place for the experiment. I bought two cheap video cameras and placed them on tree limbs in the corner of Hyde Park near the Tube station. I started them recording, walked out in the middle of the green, and jumped home to the Hole.

I returned in five minutes and left again. At ten minutes I returned, and stayed.

There were two of them, you could tell, their car came to a screeching halt in the bus lane on Kensington Road. They spread out, one coming up the main path from Queen Elizabeth's Gate and the other one cut around west, past the Boy and Dophin Fountain. They hadn't spotted me yet—I was standing next to the Rose Garden—and so it wasn't that obvious when I jumped.

I waited until they'd passed my cameras, then jumped away, west up the park toward Knightsbridge Station. They should've felt it, I hoped.

I walked across the street and into the station. After five minutes, a westbound train came through and I stepped aboard but got off, next stop, back at Hyde Park.

I strolled back casually, my eyes open for the two guys in green overcoats, but I didn't see them. I picked up the cameras and then jumped away, from the same spot I'd used before, by the Rose Garden.

One of them was blond with a receding hairline and a bald spot in back. He had almost no eyebrows and he looked familiar, but only vaguely, and I thought that perhaps he was the one who had attacked me on the stairs at the Elephant and Castle Tube stop.

I froze them on the little television screen at various points and sketched them.

His companion shaved his head, but he had dark stubble and bushy dark eyebrows and ran to fat—kind of jowly. Either of them could've been the one who'd tried at Embankment Station, when they'd snagged the two women instead—didn't see them that time. They both were Sensitives. They'd snapped their heads around the minute I'd jumped. You could see it on the tape clearly.

Must be a thankless job when your quarry can just jump away in an instant.

Then I remembered the circumstances of my first encounter. *Maybe it's not so hard, when your quarry is an inexperienced child.* Maybe they didn't have to hunt adult jumpers. Maybe the spent their time killing nine-year-olds instead. Or younger.

Now *that* would make it easier.

I had no sympathy.

I was irritated with the London police and with myself a bit, too. I should've stayed longer—as it was, the tape showed that when I jumped, the two guys had dashed back to their car to speed up Kensington after me. Not only did they not get towed or clamped, they didn't even get a ticket.

Their sketches went up on the board as London Blond and London Baldy, along with Post-its for the city and notes about where I'd seen them.

It was weird, but after I'd done this, I was able to draw a brief sketch of Sam, leaning forward, like he did on the edge of his living room couch.

Huh.

I wanted to see Alejandra, very much, but I'd insisted she just disappear, on her own, so I wouldn't know. So I couldn't betray her accidentally. Hopefully she'd discovered that she had enough money to buy a new identity—that was my hope.

I'd warned her about using her own passport—told her what happened to me in Portsmouth. She said she understood. She said not to worry. I pulled out the big gun. I told her, "Consuelo would be very angry with you if you were to come to harm."

I took a train south from Rennes, first to Bayonne, then on to Hendaye, across the Rio Bidasoa from Spanish Hondarribia. I skipped the border, using my binoculars to see across the river, then jumping to a walkway on the far bank.

Bienvenido a España.

The locals wouldn't mind my travel—they considered both sides Basque—but they probably would disagree with the "Welcome to Spain." I sat in the old quarter and sketched the wall and the castle. When the place had seeped into my bones, I walked to the train station and purchased a ticket for Madrid for the next day.

I jumped to the Hole from one of the narrow alleys.

I was exhausted but I couldn't sleep. I was thinking about Alejandra. After tossing and turning, I got up and took a fresh sketchbook over to the table, turned the lights on, and drew her.

I drew her nude, as I'd seen her under the shower in the jungle above Bahía Chacacual. I sketched for two hours. The memory was better than the sketch, but it was still the best drawing I'd ever done.

Then I was able to sleep.

The next day I talked a lot, on the train, finding interesting variations in the accent and once getting in trouble when using *taco,* which apparently means "swear word" in Spain. So much for lunch.

Because of a service problem on a train in front of us, it took six hours to get to Madrid. When I looked at the map, it surprised me that it took only that long, but going back to the scale, I realized Spain was smaller than the state of Texas.

I was still exhausted, though, from the travel and the talking and the pretending to smile—that was the most tiring. I jumped away as soon as I'd made a quick sketch of the platform itself, with the city skyline prominent.

To Whom It May Concern:

My name is Griffin O'Conner. I am the child of Robert and Hannah O'Conner, murdered on October 3rd,19——, in San Diego, CA. The accompanying sketch is of one of the three men (and one woman) involved in their murder. He was also seen in La Crucecita, Oaxaca, Mexico, on November 13th, 19——, and near the Russell Square Tube stop in London, England, March 3rd, 200—. On March 16th, 200—, he was involved with the murder of Sam Coulton and Consuelo Monjarraz y Romera and six ins agents in South-Central San Diego County, California. His name is "Kemp" and he has a pronounced English (Bristol area) accent.

Sincerely,

Griffin O'Conner, March 29th, 200—

CC: San Diego Police Department

JUMPER: GRIFFIN'S STORY

FBI, San Diego Field Office
San Diego County Sheriff's Dept.
New Scotland Yard

I reduced the sketch to half a page—I'd drawn a full-face and profile view to go with it—and put a nice inky thumbprint beside my signature, so they'd be able to prove it was really me.

I made five copies, four to send, one to put up on the board, and posted the three in San Diego, at the downtown post office on Horton Plaza, and the other in a post box outside the Epping Tube station, the very last stop on the Central line.

I went back to Mont-Saint-Michel at sunrise, jumping to the causeway, then sat and waited. If they were watching Cousin Harold they might feel me arrive; I doubted they were. But if they *had* stationed someone here, well then, they'd probably be along directly.

I just wanted to know.

I wasn't tired—I'd been shifting my operating time more to Greenwich zero. When you wake up in a sealed cave, it doesn't matter what the local sunlight is doing. I did tend to use the Kinko's in San Diego a lot but that didn't really matter, most of them were open twenty-four hours a day.

When no one arrived desperately looking for a jumper, I walked the rest of the way across the causeway to the island.

The tourist buses hadn't started arriving yet and the ones staying locally were still snug in their beds.

I received an odd look or two from the few locals who were out, but they responded with nods or smiles to my unsmiling *"bonjour."* I wanted something hot to drink, coffee preferably, but the tourist cafés weren't open yet so I found a nook and jumped to San Diego, and bought a muffin and a very large latte from a Starbucks that was about to close, then went back.

The shadows of the low morning sun threw the stonework of the spire into sharp relief and I used that, sketching the tower and the spire above from the courtyard outside the abbey. I stood up to stretch when a voice said in badly accented French, *"No! Retorner, si vous plait."* Then, immediately, in American English, *"Where* did you get Starbucks?"

I turned. A redheaded teenaged girl in an enormous black coat sat cross-legged on the stones about ten feet back near the entrance of the courtyard, a large-format sketchbook propped in her lap. The coat was tucked under her rear and legs, and she wore fingerless gloves and black-rimmed glasses, *comme* Elvis Costello. She was older than me, but still a student, I suspected. She hadn't settled into her body yet—not the way Alejandra had.

"Why shouldn't I move?" I asked her, ignoring the question about the coffee.

"You were part of the scene. I mean, I wasn't going to include you but then you didn't move for the last twenty minutes so I decided I should include you and I really like the way I got your hair and the drape of your coat so you really need to sit back down." She said this very emphatically, with a rush at the end and a stab of her forefinger at the bench where I'd sat.

I raised my eyebrows and she added with a suddenly nervous smile, "Please."

"Very well, *à votre service, mademoiselle.*" I sat back and took up the sketchpad again. "How's that?"

"Turn a little more to your left—that's it. Are you done sketching? I mean, you can go on sketching but I'm drawing you as you were looking up at the spire, the sketchpad in your lap, right?"

"I'll just look up, then—I'm done with the sketch." I could've worked on it more, but the shadows were vanishing as the sun rose higher, and part of drawing is learning when to leave off.

I was a little angry with myself. I'd been sketching for two hours, at least, and though I'd been vaguely aware of people coming and going, I hadn't been paying attention. What if it had been Kemp?

Well, it wasn't. I drank from the now cold latte but returned to the pose.

"You never said where you got the Starbucks," she said. "I thought they weren't in France."

I knew they'd been in London for a year or two but really didn't know about France. "Don't know. I got this one in San Diego." I started to look around to see how she'd take that but she stopped me.

"Be still—I'm working on your ears. You're from the States? You sound like a Brit. Long way to bring a paper cup. Why bother?"

"My parents moved around," I said, answering the first question. I decided right then to get a travel mug, to avoid this problem in the future.

"You have very distinctive ears," she said.

I blushed. "They stick out like the handles on a sugar bowl."

The girl laughed. "That's . . . sweet."

"Ha. Very funny."

"Couldn't tell it by you. Well—I'm done. I'll show you mine if you show me yours."

I raised my eyebrows again and *she* blushed.

"Sketches!"

We sat on the bench. My first impression of her coat was correct—it brushed the top of her shoes and the sleeves were rolled back once so as not to swallow her hands—a man's coat, large.

I handed her my sketchbook, open to the morning's work. She seemed surprised, then pushed hers toward me. I guess she'd meant it when she said "show," not "handle."

She was working with charcoal pencils and a kneaded eraser on nice coarse paper. More impressionistic than a study, but she was right—with just a few strokes she'd captured the way my hair was sticking up in back and the way my anorak folded as the hem rested on the bench. The tower with its spire and the courtyard walls rose nicely, too; the proportions were good and the shading of the morning light hitting the upper spire was very nice.

Looking at mine she said, "How many days have you been working on this?"

"Just this morning." I looked over at it. Mine was much more of a study, more detailed, more photorealistic, less heart. "I *was* here at sunrise."

She pointed at the stepped arches in the lower tower and the crenellations where the slate roof tiles met the granite. "It's illustration quality—I mean, I'd wouldn't be surprised at all to find it in an architecture magazine or *The New Yorker.*"

My ears—those large sugar-bowl-handle ears—burned. "Yes, but it took me two and a half hours."

"This is the sort of thing that takes some people *days.* What's your name? I want to be able to say I met you back in the day."

"Ah, well, Griffin. That's my name."

"Griffin?" She held out her hand, palm up, as if coaxing a timid animal out of a cave.

"Griffin O'Conner." Hell, I said it. It's not as if she'd be asking Interpol about me, right?

She extended the hand farther, taking mine. "Nice-tameetcha! E. V. Kelson, As in Elaine Vera Kelson, but if you want me to answer, call me E.V., okay?" She gave my hand a firm shake, then dropped it. "So, where are you staying? We're at the Auberge Saint-Pierre."

She hadn't given me back my sketchbook and was now holding it up at arm's length, comparing it with the spire itself.

"I was staying with a friend's cousin in Pontorson, but I'm leaving today." Both literal truths. Ultimately a lie.

"Oh? Me, too. We did Paris, now five days in London. What about you?"

"I'll be going back home. Uh, who is 'we'?" She looked at me blankly and I clarified, "The 'we' who're staying at the Auberge Saint-Pierre."

"Ah, the French Club. Trenton Central High School, New Jersey. There's eight girls, two boys, our teacher, and four parent chaperones."

"Ah. And do they know where you are?"

She glanced sideways at me. "Why? You planning on kidnapping me?"

I tilted my head to one side as if I were considering it, then shook my head regretfully. "I've got a bag job at noon, and two snatch-and-grabs for two-thirty. I couldn't possibly fit you in. But there's always coffee. If that would be all right with your chaperones."

"Well, yes, sort of, they know where I am—that is, on the Mont, sketching. I'm supposed to meet them back by eleven for checkout." She looked at her watch. "In two hours. If I don't get lost." She stood up promptly. "Coffee. I know where they'll serve café au lait and croissants. Found it by accident—then we can walk a bit, I'm stiff from sitting."

She took one last look at my sketch, and we exchanged books.

E.V. hated New Jersey, having moved there the previous summer from upstate New York. Her father was a chemical engineer, her mother a middle school art teacher whose jobs were always iffy as art funding was always the first thing cut. E.V.'s older brother, Patrick, was a freshman at Princeton and she had a large dog of indeterminate breed named Booger. She wanted to go to the School of Visual Arts in New York City when she graduated in two years. Her current boyfriend had asked her not to go on this trip simply because he needed her to go to a party and he was now her ex-boyfriend. "Though, to tell the truth, he was on the way out before that. He thought my *cartoons* were cute and he wanted me to draw him in the nude."

I learned all this in the ten minutes before we got to the café. Over coffee she wheedled out the fact that I was travel-ing alone and that my parents were dead.

"Oh." Her mouth opened and closed as if she was trying to find something appropriate to say.

I held up one hand. "Miss them terribly. It's been six—Oh. It's been seven years. Rather not talk about it if you don't mind. Tell me what you saw in Paris. Better yet," I tapped her sketchbook, "show me."

That worked. As I had the same sketchbook I'd had in Paris myself, we were even able to compare sketches of the same subjects.

I touched a picture of the Seine running under the Pont Neuf and said, "I love the way you did the water here near the Île de la Cité. It's alive—mine is more like asphalt than water."

"So, how often do you draw water?"

"Not often—it looks too much like asphalt."

"Practice. That's all. Make the next ten drawings you do be of water and I'll bet you catch the trick of it. Pinky deal," she said, holding out her little finger.

"Pinky deal? What do you mean?"

"You shake pinkies to seal the deal."

"How can it be a deal? What are you going to do? For your part?"

She looked at me, surprised. "Oh. I guess that's fair. But I'm telling *you* what to do. You should make the matching condition."

I thought about it. "Okay—I draw ten pictures of water and you let me draw you in London. Sunday."

"You'll be in London?"

"I can be."

"Draw me how?" she said, her eyes narrowing, and I realized she was thinking about her ex-boyfriend.

"Fully clothed, in public, but you'll have to lose the coat. Outside, say, in a park."

"We're staying at the Best Western Swiss Cottage but I have no idea where that is."

"Probably near the Swiss Cottage Tube stop—it's a

neighborhood up Camden way. That's close to Regent's Park. I'll check in with you Saturday afternoon."

"O-kay. I think we have theater tickets so don't leave it too late," she said. She took off one fingerless glove and extended her pinky, hooked it around mine, and shook it up and down firmly. She let go and said, "Now you go boom."

"What?"

"Make a fist."

I did and she crashed hers into mine and said, "Boom."

"You're insane."

She nodded emphatically. "Yes."

Phuket has amazing water, stunning shades of blue and green both still and active. I did my first sketches on Ko Bon island, moving around from the leeward side to the more active waves. I worked in Prismatic colored pencils. I rarely used color but I couldn't stand the thought of trying that transition from deeper water to shallow sand bottom with graphite alone.

Next, I tried the Thames, but it's boring in the city—row after row of apartments with water views. I went back to Oxford and dodged tourists until I found a nice spot near Magdalen Bridge where I sketched people punting through the round archways.

I thought of going back to Oaxaca but it was too painful so I spent some time at Children's Pool Beach in La Jolla drawing sea lions coming onto the sand or the waves pounding against the other side of the sheltering breakwater.

It was a gray day, overcast, and the ocean was like that, too. Graphite pencil felt right for this water. Monochrome.

Just before I left, I went to a public phone and called the San Diego FBI Field Office.

"I'd like to speak with whoever is handling the March sixteenth murder of the six INS agents."

The woman who answered the phone said, "And your name?"

"Griffin O'Conner. I sent some information last week. By mail."

"Ah. One moment, please."

I got hold music for about twenty seconds. I was going to hang up when a man came on the line. The background noise was different. "Hello? Griffin O'Conner?"

"Yes."

"Ah, good. I'm Special Agent Proctor. Give me a moment—they patched you through to my cell phone and I don't want to crash."

The background noise lessened. "There, I'm on the shoulder. Where are you?"

"Surely your office already told you the phone number and location."

Proctor was silent for a few seconds and then he chuckled. "Well, yes, they did. I got your letter. Very interesting reading."

"Has it produced any results?"

"Maybe. A lot of questions, for one thing. What makes

you think this Kemp character was involved in the murders at Sam Coulton's ranch?"

I thought about what to tell and what not to. The truth, I decided, or most of it. The only people the truth would hurt were already dead.

Or people I wished were dead.

"Kemp talked to me from there. By phone. He told me to come there or he'd kill Sam and Consuelo. I was afraid, so I called the INS and the sheriff. And yes," I added stridently, "I lied to the INS about there being a bunch of illegals there, but I thought the more people, the less chance of anyone getting—" I took a deep breath. "I lied."

"And this Kemp was there when your parents were killed?"

"Definitely."

"What's the common thread here, Griffin? What does Kemp want?"

"Me. I'm the common thread. Kemp wants me—he wants me dead."

"Why? He could've killed you at your parents', right?"

"He tried. I got away. I've got the scars."

"Again, why? What's the motive?"

I shook my head. I still didn't know—it had to have something to do with the jumping. "I don't really know why." A partial truth.

Proctor continued, "And where do Sam and Consuelo come in? Were they friends of your family? 'Cause I'm not finding any record of that."

"No. They found me in the desert after I got away. I was a mess and they took care of me until I was better. Later, I went and stayed with Consuelo's niece in Mexico, in the state of Oaxaca. Her house was blown up two weeks ago." I paused. "You knew that, right?"

Proctor exhaled. "Yeah. That I know. It was too close to the murders, the niece's home and all that. No bodies found."

"They missed. It was close."

"Were you there? There weren't any calls from Mexico that day, to the ranch."

"Ah, phone records. Mine would be the call from the pay phone in El Centro." I told him a half-truth. "Alejandra was almost killed in the explosion."

"That's the niece?"

"Yes. Alejandra Losada."

"Where is she now?"

"In hiding." I hoped. I frowned. "You haven't once asked me to come talk to you! You sent people, didn't you?"

Proctor paused, then said, "It's for your protec—"

I hung up. Out on Coast Boulevard, two black-and-white SDPD cars had stopped behind all the parked cars and four officers were getting out.

I went down the stairs past the seal observation deck, moving briskly, dodging the tourists, and headed out onto the breakwater. It was windy and cold and there were only a few people braving the sea spray that regularly shot through the railing.

The police followed slowly. It was a dead end, after all.

I reached the end, put one hand on the rail, and launched myself over. It was rocks and surf perhaps twelve feet below and I heard someone shout from behind, and then I was trembling in the Hole.

The Best Western Swiss Cottage was, oddly enough, by the Swiss Cottage Station on the Jubilee line, only a mile northwest of the zoo.

I caught E.V. in the half hour before her group was to go to dinner and a restaging of *Candide*. I called her from the house phone in the lobby.

"So, it's a pinky deal promise, right? Are we on?"

"Griffin? Ha! I told them we had a date and they said you were just putting me on. Did you keep your end of the deal?"

"You decide. I left you a packet at the front desk before I rang you up."

She gasped. "Are you here? At the hotel?"

"For a minute. I'm off to have Pakistani food in the West End. Ten o'clock all right?"

"Yes, but I've got to bring a chaperone." She said it like it was a mortal illness, like *I've got leukemia.*

"Well, that's sensible. You can't expect them to let you go off with random strangers. I mean, what do they tell your parents? 'Let her go off with a strange boy and she didn't come back. Terribly sorry.'"

She laughed. "I could come down—we're on the third, no, second floor, right? Ground, first, second?"

"Shouldn't you be getting ready for dinner?"

"Well, wait for me. They made us all dress up and somebody should see it. It's very rare for me. My mom bought this dress specifically for the trip."

I smiled. "All right, then. I'll wait down here."

The entire group, all fifteen of them, spilled down the stairs and the lifts. E.V. was wearing her gigantic black coat but unbuttoned and she spread it wide to show me a black velvet square-necked gown that more or less molded itself to her. I had to listen to a bunch of introductions while trying very hard not to stare at E.V.'s body. She was more, uh, *mature* than I'd realized, under that black coat. She still wore her glasses but her short red hair had been moussed into spikes.

I was polite to the adults and complimented the women, young and old, on their dresses. At the last minute, E.V.'s teacher, Madame Breskin, said, "We have a dinner reservation for fifteen but I wouldn't be surprised at all if they could squeeze you in, too."

"That's very kind," I said, "but I'm not really dressed for it. Perhaps another time." I offered my hand to E.V. "Take a look at the sketches. I expect a scathing critique tomorrow. Ten o'clock, in the lobby?"

She smiled and I could see her about to say something, but then her eyes darted sideways at the girls around her, and she just nodded firmly.

It was still business hours in San Diego and I decided to give Proctor another try, this time from a bank of pay phones inside Horton Plaza Mall.

"Please give me Agent Proctor's mobile phone number," I said, when the receptionist answered the phone. The woman said, "He's in the office this morning, may I connect you?"

"All right."

Proctor answered on the third ring.

"Last time I answered your questions. Now it's your turn."

"Griffin? Are you all right? They swore you must've drowned!"

I ignored that. "Did you find any trace of Kemp?"

"Maybe." Proctor paused. "What if you're working with him?"

"Give me an effing break. Who gave you him in the first place?"

"We don't disclose the details of our investigations."

"Good-bye, then."

"No, wait!"

"Give me a reason."

"We can protect you."

"That scares me more than you can imagine. Give me a real reason. Has my sketch helped?"

"I told you—"

I hung up and walked away from the bank of phones, went over to the food court and bought a gyro sandwich, then jumped away from the antechamber outside the restrooms.

I did laundry, in anticipation, washed extra hard, thick coat of deodorant, and brushed my teeth thoroughly. Twice.

She called it a date!

STEVEN GOULD

I took some deep breaths and told myself to calm down. *It's not as if you'll be alone.*

And we started out with the entire group, walking to Regent's Park, but it turned out that the majority were going to the zoo and only Madame Breskin would be tagging along with us, "if you don't walk too fast. Two weeks of touring and my feet are swelling." She tapped a book under her opposite arm. "Sitting is my goal."

When we hit the park, the rest of the group went west on the Outer Circle, headed for the zoo. We meandered down through the middle and ended up on the edge of the lake, with early rowers and the ducks, a bench for Madame Breskin, and us on the green, closer to the water.

The critique was thorough but not scathing, with examples given on the spot, in pencil, using the boating lake and the reflections of the trees.

She liked my work, though. "Didn't expect you to work from memory so much. It's really cool that you've been all these places and you remember them so well."

What could I say? After an awkward pause I tapped the Oxford drawings. "I was drawing this in the flesh. No memory involved."

"Well, I really love these pencils you did of the Bahamas."

"Uh, no—that's Thailand, near Phuket. Guess they are a bit similar, but I've never been to the Bahamas. But in *Dr. No* and *Thunderball* I guess it's similar."

"Well, are you going to sketch me?"

"Yes." I moved around a bit, considering her against the

214

available backgrounds. "Here." I settled down and took my sketchbook back. "With the gold dome of the mosque in the distance. Why don't you sit on your coat?"

The day had started out gray, with wet pavements, and I'd been afraid it would rain, but the sun and the Londoners now flooded the park. She shrugged the coat off her shoulders, revealing a tight green sweater with three-quarter sleeves and a plunging neckline. I felt my cheeks heat up.

And told myself not to stare. Well, not particularly.

"Comfortable?"

She folded her legs and leaned to the side, propped up by one elbow. "I'm set."

Madame Breskin checked on us once, saw that the work was still in progress, and went off to fetch hot chocolate from the concessionaires. The clouds were coming back again when E.V. said, "Now I'm getting cold. Since you're not drinking it, can I have some of your hot chocolate?"

I looked down, surprised. I hadn't touched it. I handed it to her. "I'm sorry, it's stone cold." I closed the sketchbook and started to stand, to help her rise, but my leg was asleep from the hip down and I fell over. As the blood started back in, I nearly screamed.

She appeared over me, alarmed. "You okay?"

"Leg's asleep," I said through clenched teeth. "Why don't you toddle off and suggest luncheon to *votre professeur, bien?*"

By the time she returned with Madame Breskin, I was on my feet, limping around in a circle.

215

The three of us went to a little Indian place in Marylebone, though I had to promise Madame Breskin that we'd return to the hotel via taxi. In a booth, she and E.V. made me show them the drawing. I winced inwardly and pushed it over, watching their heads bend together as they looked.

"Oh," said E.V. One hand reached to the neckline of her sweater and tugged it up higher. "You . . . *flatterer.*"

"My," said Madame Breskin. "I thought you were taking your time but you accomplished a *great deal* more than I expected."

Almost convulsively, E.V. said, "Look what he's done, though. I never looked like that. This girl is . . . sensual." She covered her mouth and darted her eyes sideways at her teacher.

Madame Breskin tilted her head. "Yes, I suppose. We all are, at times. If anything he's been more objective than idealistic. Sometimes we don't see what others . . . *voir d'un coup d'œil.*"

"Madame?" said E.V., preoccupied, still staring at the drawing.

Madame Breskin was regarding me and I translated, "See at a glance."

E.V. looked confused but the waiter came just then and I was relieved and E.V. was clearly relieved and Madame Breskin was clearly amused.

Later, in the lobby of the hotel, E.V. asked quietly, "I'd like a copy, if you could Xerox it."

"You can have it, when I'm done. I've just started on the

216

background. I'm not satisfied at all with the light on the mosque and the ducks, and the water—that goes without saying."

She panicked. "We're leaving in the morning! You won't have time."

"I meant, when you get back. To Trenton." I folded back the cover of the sketchbook and pointed at the blank cardboard. "Your address and phone number." I put a drawing pencil in her hand. "Please?"

"Oh. Mail." She wrote the lines neatly, elegantly. "Of course."

I shrugged.

She said, "And *your* address?"

"Post is . . . difficult where I live and I'm not on the phone. But I'll be in touch."

Madame Breskin was giving us some space. She sat in an elegant lion-footed chair by the lifts and pretended to look at her book.

I tucked the sketchbook under my arm and held out my hand. "Bon voyage, Mademoiselle Kelson."

She took my hand and said, "A handshake? Screw that." She pulled and I stepped closer. The sweater was as soft as I'd drawn it, but the lips were, if anything, softer.

"Oh!" she said. "You *can* smile."

I had to pick up the sketchbook, after, and the doorman steered me gently out onto the wet pavement past the door frame after I'd collided with it once.

It was raining, cold and nasty, but I didn't really care.

217

ELEVEN

Going for the Kidney

I was really tempted to show up at the airport the next day and surprise her but I didn't know whether they were leaving from Gatwick or Heathrow or even what airline. I must admit the phrase "leave them wanting more" went through my head but I would've gone in an instant if I just knew where and when.

I was the one wanting more.

I spent two more hours in Regent's Park, finishing up the background. I did very little to her figure—just some blending and darkening of her outline so she stood out from the background. The lace edge of a bra had shown as her neckline draped, due to gravity, and I'd drawn it faithfully, but now *it* drew *me,* my eyes returning to it, to her eyes, to her lips.

I took the drawing to a Kinko's and used their largest-format machine to produce a doubled-sized copy on art stock. Then I went to a specialty art shop to have the original matted and framed. "Your work?" said the clerk, handling it carefully by the edges. "You haven't signed it. You want me to spray it with fixative?"

Self-consciously, I signed it, first name only. Below I put "Regent's Park" and the date we'd sat there. Then he took it in the back and gave it a spritz with a can of Lascaux.

"You want it boxed, too?"

"Yes, please."

"For shipping or hand carry?"

"Hand carry—I'm going to deliver it."

The trouble was, I didn't really recall the East Coast. We'd been there when I was very young, but I just didn't remember. I bought an Amtrak train ticket for the *Southwest Chief,* leaving Los Angeles in three days and arriving in Chicago forty-two hours later. "We've got some rooms available," the clerk said.

I nodded. "Sure—that sounds good."

She looked at me, the young teen of indeterminate age, and said, "It *is* expensive. I mean, the ticket is almost eight hundred dollars more with a room."

I began counting out hundred dollar bills and she said, "Very well. Room or roomette? The roomettes don't have their own showers and toilets, but they're not as expensive."

In the end I paid a premium for the room and then again, on the *Lakeshore Limited,* for the Chicago–New York run, with a twenty-four-hour gap in between.

I wasn't going anywhere near airports—places where they wanted ID. The name I had them put on the ticket was Paul MacLand, that bastard Paully from my old karate class.

I gave Special Agent Proctor one more chance, again catching him at his desk.

"One last chance," I told him from a pay phone near Balboa Park. "You want my cooperation or not?"

He made a slight concession. "I'll answer your questions face-to-face. Not over the phone."

"Where?" I seriously considered it. After all, it wasn't as if he could hold me.

"Here—in my office."

"Bugger that!" I bit my lip. "I might consider someplace else. Balboa Park, perhaps? You could be there in ten minutes, right?"

"Maybe."

"You'd have to come alone."

"What, alone and unarmed?" You could cut the scorn with a knife.

"Bring as many guns as you want. Just be alone."

Pause. "I've got a call scheduled. How about forty-five minutes?"

He was stalling. "Take it on your cell on the way here."

"It's the deputy director. I can't."

"I did mention that this is your *last* chance, right?"

"But I really can't! Maybe I could cut it down to thirt—"

I cut him off. "I won't be calling again." And hung up.

The next morning I jumped to Universal Studios in L.A., a place I'd been with Mum and Dad. Saw the shark. I left immediately, overwhelmed by the memories.

Why should happy memories hurt more than the images in my head from *that* night?

I caught the brand-new Red Line extension at Hollywood and Vine and rode it all the way to Union Station. My train didn't leave until the next evening, but I wanted a jump site. I sketched the funky Mission-style clock tower from outside.

Back in San Diego I called the sheriff's department from an office phone in the county courthouse. The office was empty for lunch and the door was locked but it was glass and I could see through it. The Central Investigations Division at the main office gave me a cell phone number. "Detective Vigil is coordinating with the federal authorities." She used the Spanish pronunciation, Vee-hill.

I tried the number and after five rings a voice said, "Bob Vigil."

"My name is Griffin O'Conner, Detective. I sent a sketch to your department."

There was a sharp intake of breath. "Really. That's odd. The Feds seem to think you're in Europe."

Huh. The U.K. Immigration Service was talking to the FBI? Maybe through New Scotland Yard? "You got caller ID?"

"Yeah. I see you're local right now."

"Any luck with the sketch? Was it helpful?"

"Shit, yes! The car rental company ID'd him, the guy whose car they stole in Mexico ID'd him. The Azteca Airlines clerk at Rodrìguez ID'd him."

"Rodrìguez? Where's that?"

"Tijuana," said Vigil. "General Abelardo L. Rodrìguez International Airport."

"Where'd he fly?"

"They don't know. She doesn't remember and the ID he used apparently wasn't for 'Kemp.' That name wasn't on any of their manifests. Flights left for several cities both in and out of Mexico. The FBI are trying for security video on the departing flights in Tijuana and arriving flights at the possible cities."

"Does Special Agent Proctor at the San Diego FBI office know this?"

"That's who told me."

Bastard.

Vigil continued, "We surmise that Sam didn't have a phone number for you—that's why the perp's camped out there, right?"

"Camped out? At Sam's place?"

"Yeah—they were there a good week. It ties into the car rental and the amount of trash they generated. I take it that Sam couldn't just call you."

I winced. "Uh, no. I called him. I'm semiregular, but—" *God.* They'd held Sam and Consuelo for an *entire week* waiting for me to call? I felt like throwing up. I wanted to race to Paris and search until I found Alejandra, to protect her.

You'd just lead them to her.

Vigil interpreted my silence. "You see it, eh?"

My breathing deepened. "Yes!"

He was tactfully quiet for a moment.

After my breathing calmed I said, "Anybody else? Have you figured how many there were?"

"Paolo saw four. He's the guy who was carjacked on Highway Two. We have some pictures of them, from the camera at the rental place. You could take a look and see if you recognize them."

"Do you have Kemp in those shots?"

"No. According to the rental agent he stayed outside. One of these other guys took care of the paperwork."

I suppose he could be one of the guys I'd encountered in the London Tube, or the Big Man in Oaxaca. My train wasn't going to leave for another twenty-six hours. "I guess I could come look. Where are you?"

223

"I'm at Lemon Grove substation. Your number looks like its downtown, yes?"

"I'm at the county courthouse."

"I'm going to the main office. I could meet you someplace closer to downtown."

Well, he had answered my questions, unlike Proctor, and I wanted to see the pictures—the other faces.

"Okay. The main library on E Street."

"Right. Take me twenty-five minutes, okay? Just inside?"

"Sure. Are you in uniform?"

"No. I'll have a red folder with the pictures—I'll wave it. I'm Hispanic, about two hundred pounds, and I've got on a brown suit, no tie. Clean-shaven. Well, I was this morning."

"Right."

I jumped to the little staff parking lot behind the central branch library and walked around to the front. For a moment I stood under the covered entranceway on the sidewalk, looking around, but it was just a busy San Diego weekday. I went inside and found a place where I could watch the door from behind a circular book display rack and lean against a wall.

Lots of people moved in and out through the doors in the next thirty minutes. Finally, as advertised, a man in a brown suit came in, a thick red file folder in his hand. He was holding it in front of him chest high.

I pushed off the wall and went to meet him. As I passed the reference books I heard a step and twisted to my left to see a man lunge out from between the shelves. Something flashed in his hand and I felt a pressure on my back ribs, then excruciating pain. His hand, and the flashing metal, came back for another stroke, toward my stomach, and I was gone.

I staggered across the uneven floor of the Hole and fell to one knee. When I tried to lift my left hand to feel back there, I screamed, and dropped it again. Where my arm rested against my leg, I could feel the cloth was soaked. I couldn't even twist to look down but I tilted my hand and saw blood on the fingers.

I needed a doctor, urgently, before I bled to death, but I also needed to avoid the places I frequented. Going to hospital in London could be quickly fatal. Definitely in San Diego, too, or the clinic I knew in La Crucecita. I managed to stand though the effort caused my sight to darken and the room to spin. I found myself staring at my sketches, pinned to the sheets of plywood.

There.

It was early evening in Hondarribia, but the old quarter was well lit, and when I sprawled facedown on the pavement, the red mess on the back of my pale shirt apparently stood out very well, for the last thing I heard was a woman screaming and a man's voice saying, *"¡Por la sangre de Cristo!"*

Indeed.

I woke up lying on my stomach, my head tilted to one side. My back didn't hurt as much but someone was tugging on it. I started to shift and a hand pressed down on my shoulder. A man's voice said, *"¡ No te muevas! ¿Entiendes?"*

I settled back down. *"Entiendo."* After a minute I asked where I was. *"¿Dónde estoy?"*

"Mi clínica. Soy el doctor Uriarte. El policía te trajo."

The police brought me, eh? I thought about what was in my pockets. Just money. English pounds, some francs, some U.S. dollars. Maybe an art eraser. No ID—not since my passport had been confiscated by UK Immigration.

"Treinta-nueve puntadas," Dr. Uriarte announced. *"Por todo."*

Thirty-nine stitches. He'd obviously numbed it but my imagination made it itch and ache and tingle all at once. He dressed it.

He helped me to sit. I was naked. My shirt, pants, underwear, my shoes, my socks, were all in a corner, in a bloody pile—even my shoes had blood on them. I had an IV in my left arm, some clear fluid running down the tube. The room spun and he kept his hands on my shoulders until I said, *"Bien."*

He put a dressing on and fastened it by taping all the way around my ribs, watching me carefully to make sure I didn't fall over. *"¿Usted recuerda ser atacado?"*

Well, yes, I did remember being attacked but I shook my head. *"No. Sucedió muy rápido."* It happened too fast.

He took a plastic bag from the far counter and started to hand it to me. *"Tenga su dinero*—are you American?" He'd noticed the dollars. His English was thickly accented but colloquial.

"British," I said.

"Oh. Your Spanish sounds like Mexico."

I nodded. "Yeah—that's where I learned it."

"I went to school in Texas," he said. "Baylor Medical School."

"Ah. I've lived in California. I'm a little cold, Doctor."

"Oh, forgive me." He pulled a cabinet open and took out an examination robe. "I'm a pediatrician. My clinic is near where you were mugged and I live next to it. I'm afraid I stitch up a lot of the local bar fighters." He took out the IV and helped me put on the robe. "What hotel are you staying at?"

"None. Only just arrived."

"Oh, so they stole your passport. I was hoping it was at your hotel."

I shook my head.

"The nearest British consul is in Bilbao. I think they can issue emergency passports."

I nodded.

"You need to be very careful—I stitched together three different layers of muscle. No exercise for four weeks, and then some physiotherapy." He pursed his lips. "It could've been much worse. I think they were going for your kidney. You would've died within minutes."

I remembered twisting around at his movement. *Yeah, he missed.* But if he hadn't, it wouldn't matter how fast I'd jumped? "I would've bled to death?"

"Oh, yes. The renal artery is very big. Only immediate attention in a trauma center could have saved you. Your attacker must've been a very desperate man."

I blinked. "I'm not feeling much."

"Oh, you will. You'll need something for the pain. I'll write you a script."

"And the stitches?"

"Ten days. The internal ones will dissolve—don't worry about them."

"Okay."

"If there is redness or discharge or swelling, get to a hospital."

"Okay. How much do I owe you?"

"You don't have insurance?"

"No."

He told me how much he would've been charged against an insurance company and I gave him that and half again in the U.S. dollars.

"The police are waiting to talk to you."

"Of course," I said.

I asked to use his bathroom and didn't come out.

At first, I slept well, but the lidocaine faded and pain brought me awake, a shout of pain echoing off the walls of the Hole. It was agony to put a T-shirt on. Merely painful to pull on some shorts.

I jumped to a *farmacia* in La Crucecita. I didn't care if the bastards detected the jump—you don't need prescriptions to get pain medication in Mexico. I explained my problem to the pharmacist, even started to lift my shirt to show the dressing, but raising my left arm was not in the cards.

The pharmacist looked alarmed at my expression and gestured for me to put the shirt back down. *"¿Treinte-nueve puntadas?"* The number of stitches really impressed him.

"Verdad."

He sold me a bottle of Tylenol with codeine. I jumped back to the Hole before I was through the door.

I wasn't able to get back to sleep but the ache died to a dull throbbing. I dressed carefully and shopped for new shoes, first in San Diego, then in Rennes. Had to let the clerk tie them for me. At six that evening I carefully boarded the *Southwest Chief* at Los Angeles' Union Station, let the conductor show me to my expensively exclusive room, and, with the aid of the pills, slept fitfully on my right side.

My plan had been to sketch at every stop along the way, but the drugs knocked me (and that plan) on its ass. I did manage a few drawings out the stateroom window at the stations in Kingman, Flagstaff, and Winslow. In New Mexico I got Albuquerque, Lamy, and Raton, but I doubled up on the pills after that and slept all the way through Colorado and most of Kansas, waking up in time to sketch Lawrence and Kansas City. There was only one other stop in Missouri, La Plata, and only one in the corner of Iowa before we began crossing Illinois. I gave up drawing. Everything hurt too much and the pills were making me constipated.

The last five hours into Chicago were misery encased in a fuzzy drug fog. I stank—I hadn't trusted my ability to keep the stitches dry and just washing my armpits was surprisingly difficult. I'd been bumped by other passengers several times as I tottered along the passageway to the dining car.

And I'd been thinking.

He'd told them. Investigator Vigil had told them I'd be at the library. They'd been waiting. They'd either gotten there ahead of me or come in a different entrance, possibly circumventing the emergency exit alarms.

But Vigil had told them.

Bastard.

I checked into a hotel near the station, paying in advance. I explained that I'd been mugged and that was why I didn't have any ID. Looking at my face in the mirror later, I looked older than I remembered. I *was* older, but the real change stemmed from the pain. Maybe they thought I was over eighteen or maybe they just felt sorry for me.

I used the bathtub, gratefully, leaving my left arm down, the water shallow. I managed to get rid of the stink and even wash my hair a bit. The bed was softer than mine back in the Hole, but even with the drugs, every noise brought me awake with an adrenaline rush. Finally, I turned on the lights, got a good look at the room, and jumped back to the Hole, where, harder bed or not, I actually slept for six hours.

That was when I turned the corner, I think.

It hurt the next morning but not so bad. It was manageable.

I didn't take a pill, and by the time I'd finished breakfast back in the Chicago hotel, the drug-induced haze was lifting.

The *Lakeshore Limited* left at 7:55 P.M. and arrived at Penn Station midafternoon the next day. I'd slept better than I had since the attack and as soon as I was off the train I bought a New Jersey Transit ticket for Trenton. While I waited for the 5:01 train, I drew a nook under the Seventh Avenue steps. The train was ridiculously crowded, but then it was rush hour. It hurt to sit, anyway, so I found a corner where I could prop myself without leaning against the stitches.

The trip was just over an hour.

Trenton was wet, light rain.

The concessionaire had a Trenton map. Trenton Central High School, where E.V. went, was about a half mile from the station and her address, on Euclid Avenue, was even closer.

But it was raining and an hour standing on the train had wiped me like a blackboard. I sketched a spot on Platform 1D, complete with scurrying commuters, and jumped back to the Hole.

Ten days after the attack, I went back to Dr. Uriarte, waiting with mothers and their sick kids in his pediatric waiting room.

He blinked when he saw me, puzzled, and then he remembered. "*¡Es usted!* Where did you go?" He looked around at the interested audience and waved me back to his examining rooms. Several women who'd been there before me looked murderous.

When he'd closed the door to the examining room he said, "The police were very upset with me. They said I was lying when I told them you'd left, naked."

"*Lamento mucho.* I didn't mean for them to bother you. I need my stitches out, but if it would cause trouble, I could find someplace else. I'll pay cash."

He considered it. "Of course we'll take out your stitches. They didn't *say* to call if you came back."

"Ah. *Muchas gracias.*"

He had one of his nurses pull them while he dealt with some of the other patients and their angry mothers, but he came back and examined the cut when she was done. "Excellent. There will always be a scar. A line, but I think you won't have any functional damage."

I paid him twice what he said the amount was.

I called on a Friday night, from Penn Station. She wasn't at home but her mother told me she'd be back by ten and she was, snatching up the phone when it rang at 10:05 P.M.

"Hello?"

"Hello, E.V., it's—"

She interrupted. "It *is* you. I've been waiting almost an hour! My mother could've called me—I was just down the block at Rhonda's! She didn't realize it had to be an overseas call!"

232

"Well, no. Actually not. I'm in New York City."

She was quiet for a second then said, "Really?"

"Really. I was wondering if I could drop off that sketch, tomorrow, perhaps, if your schedule is clear."

She laughed. "Clear. Mother? Is my 'schedule' clear tomorrow?" She said it British, like I had, "shed-youl." "Of course my schedule is clear." This time she said it with the hard *c*. "Where? When? Should I take a train into the city?"

I liked that idea a lot but I said, "No. Don't think your parents would give that a go, would they? Better I should come to you. All right if I come around about ten? Euclid Avenue, right? Looks like it's walking distance from the station."

"How'd you know that?"

"Maps, m'dear. Maps."

"Oh. Well, that would be fine. What are you doing in New York?"

"Talking to you."

I jumped to the Trenton station the next morning and joined the crowd getting off a Philadelphia train. I walked, stretching my legs more and more. The cut was still incredibly sore but I was regaining my stamina. I no longer got dizzy standing up, and I was able to manage the boxed sketch under my right arm. For the first time in two weeks, I felt clean, having had an excellent shower—no worries about getting the stitches wet.

There were buds just beginning on the trees and green grass sprouting among last year's brown. Her home was a yellow-brick two-story with an enclosed porch. She'd called

233

it a "colonial" on the phone. She was on the stairs when I turned onto the block, though she waited until I was in her yard before advancing to meet me. I could tell she was going to try to hug me, so I held out the box, quickly, and she had to halt her advance to take it.

"Come in, come in."

Both her parents were waiting in the front parlor. Her mother was standing by the window and her dad was seated, with a book, but I had the feeling they'd both been waiting. I put on my best manners as I was introduced.

"Pleasure to meet you. Charmed."

Mrs. Kelson was a redhead but running to silver. Mr. Kelson wore his dark hair cut seventies-long, over the ears, over the forehead. It hadn't gone gray yet or there was dye involved. I didn't like his smile—it didn't touch his eyes.

It may have been a "who are you and what are you doing with my daughter" thing.

Her mum's smile was genuine, though. Mrs. Kelson loved the sketch. E.V.'s dad said "very nice," but his brow was furrowed and he stole surreptitious looks from the sketch to his daughter and back.

"You made a copy?" E.V. asked.

"Yeah, I've got a decent photocopy." I didn't say it was twice the size of the original and hung beside my bed. I didn't think that would go over so big—not with her father.

"What are you doing in New York, Griffin?" asked Mr. Kelson.

"On my way home from Europe. I live in Southern Cal."

"Oh, really? Not England?" He looked at his daughter.

"We didn't really discuss it, Daddy. I saw him in London and he's British. What was I supposed to think?"

"Yeah," I added. "We were talking about drawing, mostly."

"Where in Southern California?"

"Out in the desert, in west San Diego County. The nearest town is called Borrego Springs." This was the truth, after all, but then I lied. "I spend half the time with my uncle in California, the other half in Lechlade, in Oxfordshire, with my grandparents. I was visiting a friend's cousin when I met E.V. in France."

"Your schooling must be complicated," Mrs. Keslon said.

"I'm on self-study. Homeschooling. It's the only way this works. When I go to university, it'll be different."

E.V. turned to face her parents. She said, "I'm taking Griffin to Laveta's for coffee."

"We've got coffee here—" That furrow between Mr. Kelson's eyebrows was back again but Mrs. Kelson cut in, saying quickly, "Certainly. Are you going to get lunch out, or would you like to eat with us? Patrick's coming in from Princeton on the train."

E.V. glanced at me then said, "My brother. We'll catch him after lunch, okay?"

"Okay," Mrs. Kelson said. "He's going back on the four-seventeen so make sure you get back in time."

"Right," said E.V.

She grabbed her coat—the large black one she'd worn in Europe—and shrugged into it and we were out the door.

"Walking?" I asked.

"Yeah, it's close. Over on State Street, near the train station but on the far side." She grabbed my left arm and I tensed and she let go. "What's wrong? Is that not okay?"

Her face had dropped as if I'd struck her and I hurried to reassure her. "Sorry—hurt my back. It's the left side. I'd love for you to hold my other arm, though."

He relief was palpable. "I thought you were moving a little stiffly."

"Yeah."

It took ten minutes to walk to Laveta's, where we got coffee to go. Behind the coffee shop a cemetery stretched between State Street and the train station. "You warm enough?" she asked. It had started partially cloudy but now it was completely overcast and the wind was gusting around corners with a moist bite.

"Maybe if you let me share your coat."

She grinned. "I like the way you think."

She showed me a bench in the back corner of the graveyard. "Here. I come here to sketch." She opened her coat wide on the bench and invited me to sit on it. When I did, she wrapped it around us both.

"Huh," she said.

I barely dared breath. "What?"

"We both fit in here just fine. I thought you were larger. You take up more space in my mind."

"Sorry. Always been short for my—"

She kissed me.

I closed my eyes and leaned into it.

After a moment she drew back and I said, "You could've just said shut up."

"Are you complaining? I mean—"

This time *I* stopped her mouth with a kiss.

Oh. My.

Hands were roaming, mine, hers, hers guiding mine. I ached and not in the bad way of the last two weeks. Her hand, roaming up under my shirt, found the cut and I nearly yelled in her ear.

"I'm sorry. They took out the stitches yesterday and it's still, uh, tender."

"Stitches? What happened?"

We'd ended up apart. She turned me around and lifted the edge of my jacket and shirt, previously tucked in, now out. "Jesus Christ! What happened?"

My mouth worked but nothing came out.

"Griffin? What's wrong? Someone did this to you, didn't they?"

"Well, yeah," I said.

"Why? That's from a knife, right?"

"Yeah, it is." Then, in a rush, "He was aiming for my kidney." I stood up and let the jacket and shirt drop back down. "Cold."

She pulled her coat closed.

"Who did that?"

237

"I lied to your parents."

She looked confused. "What? Can't you answer a straight question? What do you mean, you lied to my parents?"

"I don't live with my uncle or my grandparents. I don't have grandparents. I don't have an uncle. After my parents were—after they died—I lived with a friend in Mexico, then later, I got my own place. The place in the desert I talked about—that part was real."

"What's that have to do with the cut on your back?"

I kicked at a pile of last fall's leaves, clumped and decomposing, sending them flying. It was a mistake. "Ow!" I limped around in a little circle, favoring my left side. "What I'm trying to say is that I don't want to lie to you. But I don't want to be thought crazy, too, and some of the stuff I want to say sounds terribly crazy."

She pulled her legs up onto the bench under the coat, and hugged them. "What kind of crazy?"

"The people who killed my parents are still trying to kill me. They were trying to kill me when they killed them."

She looked like she was about to cry. *She doesn't believe me. She does think I'm insane.* I held out my hand like a crossing guard stopping oncoming traffic. "Wait. There's proof."

And I jumped away.

She's going to run screaming, I thought, as I ripped the old microfilm newspaper printouts from my plywood gallery.

I jumped back.

She was standing, but she hadn't run. She did have her fist against her mouth. She flinched back and sat down hard as the concrete bench caught the backs of her knees. She began gasping.

I took a step closer and her eyes widened and she leaned away. Well, now I knew how she'd felt when I'd flinched away from her in front of her house, when she'd grabbed my left arm and hurt my back by accident. I moved very slowly and set the papers down on the end of the bench but the minute I let go, the wind threatened to send them flying and I dropped my hand back down.

"Look, they're gonna be all over if you don't take them." I slid them closer to her, careful to stay beyond the end of the bench.

She put her hand down, as far from my hand as possible and yet still on the pages. I straightened up and backed away.

"What was that?" There was suppressed hysteria in her voice. "How did you do that?"

I gestured to the papers. "It ties in. Go ahead, look."

When she'd picked them up I said, "I've got other cuts— older scars," I said quietly. "The top two stories are when they came for me when my parents were alive. I know it says drugs were involved but that was bullshit." I pointed to my right hip, the wound I got that night. "They nearly killed me that night."

She read through the pages, glancing up often to keep track of where I was. "So your name really is Griffin O'Conner."

When she got to the third page she said, "Who's Sam Coulton and Consuelo, uh, Mon-jarraz?" She got the *j* right, a soft *h*.

"Sam and Consuelo found me in the desert after . . . that night. They fixed me up. Later, Consuelo took me to Oaxaca and I lived with her niece for almost two years, until *they* found me again and I had to leave. After that, I lived by myself.

"They held Sam and Consuelo hostage, trying to get me to surrender. When I sent the INS in . . . well, you see what happened."

She read on. She stopped tracking me as she got into the body count. I crossed my right arm over my stomach, pulling my left into my side. I felt my shoulders droop, hunch forward. *The accused is in the dock awaiting the verdict of the jury.*

"So why do they want to kill you?"

I shook my head. "I wish I knew for sure."

"It's something to do with, uh, what you just did, right?"

"Yeah—I really think so."

"And what *did* you just do?" She licked her lips. "I mean, I saw you disappear, but where did you go?"

"My place—uh, Southern Cal. In the desert."

"You're kidding me."

I shook my head. "No. Want to see?" I took a step forward. She held up her hands. "Whoa, boy!"

I stepped back again, the corners of my mouth tugging down. *Please, please, please.*

She pointed at the far side of the cemetery. "See the corner over by the birth control clinic?" It was about two hundred yards away. "Go there. Show me."

I did.

How many Sensitives could there be? Hopefully there wasn't one around here.

I stood there, two hundred yards away, and waved. After a moment, she raised her arm and made a large come-here gesture. I returned, my way. She didn't jerk so much this time when I appeared.

"I suppose it could be drugs. Did you put something in my coffee?"

I shook my head.

"How do you do that?"

"I just do it. When I was five, the first time."

"The Starbucks cup, in Mont-Saint-Michel—you said you'd got it in San Diego. You meant *that* morning, didn't you?"

I nodded.

It started to rain, fat drops falling at an angle with the wind.

"Shit!" said E.V. "I'm so tired of winter! I want it to be warm." She sounded upset and I didn't think it was the weather.

"I can't make it warm here," I said. "But I can take you someplace that is."

She didn't say no. Her eyes were still wary but her forehead was no longer furrowed.

"How do you feel about Thai food?"

TWELVE

Rites of Passage

We were walking down Kensington High Street on our third date when E.V. said, "Let's go in here."

I thought she meant the shoe boutique but she pulled me sideways toward the shop on the corner.

"What? The chemist?"

"Yes, the chemist."

I followed her through the door—it was afternoon in New Jersey and nearly ten at night in London and they were about to close. "What do you need?"

She looked over her shoulder at me and said, "What do *we* need." Then she blushed.

She bought the condoms, Durex brand, and some lubricant but got the cash from me since she only had American.

The clerk looked bored and my ears burned.

Back on the sidewalk she said, "We've two more hours."

I'd offered to show her my place, the Hole, before, but she'd refused. So far she'd let me take her swimming in Mexico, to Paris for coffee, to Madrid for tapas, and Phuket for satay. But not to my place.

"Uh, I've never done it."

She nodded. "I know. I could tell." She stepped up to me and pressed against me. "Don't you want to?"

I nodded mutely.

"Well, then."

It was after, when we were lying in my bed, hip to belly, that she finally found out I was thirteen months younger than her seventeen and a half years.

"Oh, Christ! It's like child abuse!"

I moved my hand sideways and she arched her back. "Well, more fun than self-abuse," I said. "Think of it as charity to a poor orphan boy."

"An orphan boy?"

"An orphan boy."

She sang,

> *"Oh, men of dark and dismal fate,*
> *Forgo your cruel employ,*
> *Have pity on my lonely state,*
> *I am an orphan boy!"*

"Huh?" I was thoroughly confused.

"And you an Englishman! *Pirates of Penzance.* Gilbert and Sullivan. Got it?"

"Oh. Never saw it. 'Modern Major-General,' right? Okay, have pity on my lonely . . . ?"

"State. What time is it? Oh, shit!" She pushed my hands away. "Get me back or I'll be grounded for all time."

I jumped her to the corner of her block, depending on the gathering gloom to hide our sudden appearance. She kissed me and ran up the block, her book bag thumping at her shoulder.

I walked between two parked cars on the street and jumped away.

E.V.'s father had a rough commute, forty-five minutes, so he was rarely home before six. Her mother worked in a middle school in the Neshaminy school district in Pennsylvania— across the river and then some. She rarely made it home before five-thirty. So we had that time between three-fifteen and five-thirty, most weekdays.

"I'm not burning us out, though," she said. "Three times a week, tops."

I had to buy more condoms.

She drew me naked.

Well, naked with a sketchpad.

We drew each other.

And we swam naked in the moonlight at Phuket.

And we ate at little cafés overlooking the Seine while she did her class assignments. I helped her with her French—she helped me with Algebra II.

"Madame Breskin says my accent is improving remarkably."

"*Le français est la langue de l'amour.* Let's go back to my place."

She laughed. "No. I've barely got time to finish this essay."

My sigh was eloquent.

"Tomorrow. Homework or not," she promised.

But the next day she wasn't there. We'd been meeting at the Shell station, across Greenwood Avenue from the high school and only a few blocks from her house.

I thought about calling but she told me her parents had caller ID, so if I was going to call, do it from where I was supposed to be. With a small mountain of quarters, I stood at a pay phone in San Diego's Balboa Park, and dialed.

She answered. "Hey," I said.

"Where are you calling from? Ah, where's six-one-nine?"

"San Diego. How are you?" What I really meant was, *Can you talk?*

"I'm pissed. Dad went through my nightstand. He found the sketch I did of you in the nude. When we were sketching?"

245

"That was a really good sketch. Uh, what did he say? What did *you* say?"

"I said I'd drawn it from my imagination. Also that it was none of his business and if he ever went through my stuff again, I'd leave home." She cleared her throat. "There was some shouting involved."

"When did this happen?"

"Today. He showed up and pulled me out of school last period. Sorry. I'm grounded for a month. He suspects something—I have to come straight home after school and check in with him by phone at work. Can't go anywhere. He'll probably spot check with phone calls."

"What are you going to do?"

"I'll stick it out. My mother's upset, but a bit more at him, I think. I know *they* did it in high school. He's a hypocrite. She's the one who made sure I had condoms when I entered high school."

"Oh, yeah? I knew I liked her." I tried to keep my voice light but I felt like crying. I couldn't imagine not seeing her for an entire month.

"Yeah. We fought like wildcats when I was in middle school but we've come to a pretty good place now. But I'm not speaking to Dad. I predict two weeks, tops, then he'll cave. Maybe even sooner."

That wasn't quite as bad. "Will I be able to call you?"

"Hmmm. I don't see why not. We've got call waiting. He'll know you called, though—he'll check the numbers when he gets home—so make sure it's from San Diego, right?"

"Right."

I heard a noise in the background. "They're calling me for supper. Gotta go."

"Okay. *Je t'aime.*"

"Damn straight," she said.

I did laundry. The sheets needed changing. I bought more sheets, a nicer comforter, more pillows. She'd complained about my not having music, so I bought a large portable stereo, one that could run off my twelve-volt power system, and a selection of CDs. I stocked up on her favorite diet cola and some snacks, healthy and otherwise. She liked those weird rice cakes, the ones that are like Styrofoam, so I bought a case of those.

I bought a better portable toilet for my bathroom nook, one that used chemicals to keep the smell down. I could still dump it in the same pit toilet at the park picnic area and it had a nicer seat.

I added two more solar water heaters for the shower back in Oaxaca.

Well, that killed three days.

My side was getting better. While no longer tender, it pulled when I moved my upper body, so I began doing some stretches.

I bought a heavy bag and a stand for it, but it wasn't stable on the uneven floor of the cave, so I ended up setting it in concrete. After a few days of hitting this, I also went back to the *makiwara* in the Empty Quarter. One of them had been

247

taken, maybe used for firewood, and I had to reset a couple of the others that had come loose in the soil.

My left side was weak, the tugging from the scar profound. I doubled up on that side, both the stretches and the strikes, and there was some improvement.

I talked to E.V. every weekday afternoon.

"Now he's even more suspicious. He's wondering why you weren't calling before and now you are."

"Oh, great. Should I stop?"

"Hell, no! But if this keeps up, I'm thinkin' you might join me in the afternoons. I mean, *I've* got a bed."

"I've never been in your room. In fact, it was only that one day that I was in your house—when I brought the sketch—and then later, when I met Patrick and Booger."

"Yeah? What does that mean?"

"I can't jump without a clear memory. I mean, I can jump someplace I can see, but otherwise I really need to be familiar with it. That's why I have all those sketches."

"Hmm. Well, I'm really getting desperate, if you know what I mean."

"Believe me, I *know*."

At three weeks, her father relented.

I met her at our usual spot and we went straight to the Hole. She approved of the pillows and the comforter and the toilet but I don't think she noticed until after the second time.

"Oh, God. I needed that. Boy, did I need that." She poked at my arm. "You've been exercising."

"Yeah. Especially my right arm."

We showered together in Oaxaca, washing each other slowly. The temperature was just right.

After we were dressed, we sat in the sun on the beach below, me on a rock and her in the sand at my feet. I brushed her hair until it was dry.

I left her in our corner of Mercer Cemetery. I wanted to walk her home but she kissed me and said, "No. Not when you're supposed to be in San Diego. See you Thursday!"

She was there on Thursday but pale.

"What's wrong?"

"Oh, I've got a headache," she said. "But I've also got some good news. I told them I'd be out until nine. Some friends of mine are playing the Teen Club. We're to lend moral support. They're not that good a band but they play really loud."

I was stunned by the good fortune. "That's almost six hours!"

"Well, we do have to actually go to the club—but I don't intend to get there until seven at the earliest." She looked anxious. "That okay?"

"You're not worried someone will see me and tell your parents?"

"I want to dance with you."

"Have you *seen* me dance? Anyway, we can find places to dance far from Trenton."

She shook her head. "I *want* us to go."

"*¡Claro que si!* At your command. And what do we do before then?"

"I don't know about you, but I want to screw."

There was something wrong. She was clinging to me hard, almost desperately.

"Are you all right?"

"Don't stop!" She buried her face in my chest and pulled me hard against her. The lights were dim but it seemed like her eyes were wet. She dug her nails into my back and I forgot everything but moving.

When she came it was loud, almost anguished, great shuddering gasps, and what little control I had went with it. I was drowsy and she pulled my head onto her shoulder. "Sleep. This once, we've got the time."

I thought it might still be her dad. It must be hard to have to lie to your parents. I worried for a moment that it might be *me* but she was holding me close and stroking my back.

She woke me again later and we made love once more, long and lingering. Then she looked at her watch and said, "Fuck. Quick shower?"

The sun was low in Oaxaca but the water was still warm and "quick" was the word, for the mosquitoes were coming out.

The Teen Club was nearer the Delaware River, but still walkable, and while it was cold in Trenton, it wasn't as cold as it had been the week before. I was wearing my anorak but the minute we'd paid our cover and got inside, I took it off and carried it because the club, either from too much central heat or too many occupants, was like an oven, worse than Oaxaca.

Many of these kids clearly didn't use deodorant.

The band *was* loud and they weren't terrible—three guys on drums, guitar, and bass, and three girls on vocals. They tended toward punk with industrial overtones and either the club had a full light setup or these kids had way too much money. There were strobes and motorized track lights and lasers and a smoke machine.

Conversation was barely possible if you shouted or if you timed your sentences in the gaps. They sold refreshments but no alcohol. Most of the customers were under twenty-one but some weren't, and there were chaperones, leaning against the walls, eyes moving restlessly. One of them had his fingers plugged firmly into his ears.

There were tables around the edge but they were all taken, either occupied or piled high with coats. I yelled in E.V.'s ear, "Why don't I drop our coats back at my place?"

"What?"

It took two more efforts to make her understand. "Oh! Okay." She took her pocketbook and something else out of her coat pockets before pushing the coat into my arms.

I wandered back toward the bathrooms, looking for an unoccupied corner, but there were kids making out in the dark hallway. The bathroom itself, though, was empty, and I jumped carefully.

To return I jumped back to an empty lot we'd crossed walking here. There was a streetlight but it had been smashed and I'd remembered being a little uncomfortable taking E.V. that route, picking my way across the junk-strewn ground.

By myself, I didn't care, even when I saw three guys moving from the edge of the lot into the middle, to block my way. I kept walking straight at them and when one of them lifted a pipe in his hand and said, "Stop," I just jumped past them, to the sidewalk at the corner.

One of them yelled and another was saying, "What the fuck!" over and over and over. I looked back and saw that they'd turned, perhaps having heard my footsteps on the walk, but they were making no move to follow.

I was still grinning when I showed the man at the door the stamp on my hand.

E.V. was standing near the refreshment bar juggling two drinks and her pocketbook. The dancing had spread and she was having a hard time keeping the drinks safe from flying arms and jumping bodies. She was watching the back hallway to the bathrooms, the direction I'd left, and her face was anxious, as if she was afraid I wouldn't come back or something.

I tapped her shoulder and she jumped. I'd swear she screamed but the music was so loud, it may have been just a gasp. Both drinks hit the floor, though, together, spraying my legs and hers.

I did hear her say "Fuck!" quite distinctly—it was one of those lulls in the music. "Sorry, sorry." She started to reach down but I caught her shoulder and stopped her. The floor was already littered with paper cups stamped flat by the dancers.

The band reached the end of one number and the drummer and the lead vocalists were discussing something off mike. In the momentary silence I said, "What are we drinking?"

"I got you a Sprite. You know what I had. And I dropped them both! Whatever you want."

I managed to place the order just before the band started up. Payment was successfully accomplished with hand signs. I delivered her diet soda and tried my coffee. It was in a Styrofoam cup, too hot to drink and, in this environment, potentially disastrous. First- or second-degree burns, I thought, and turned suddenly back toward the bar to get some cream or ice to cool it down.

He was older than the kids around him, dressed grunge, but he'd been stepping forward when I saw him, his left hand held out slightly, chest high, his other hand held low by his leg. He lunged as the stage strobes were flashing and the knife cut upward in discrete stop-motion steps.

I stepped back, bumping someone dancing, and threw the coffee straight out. He jerked back, clawing at his face and

shirt. There was other movement, sudden, not the puzzled re-
action of bystanders but deliberate motion among the dancers,
and I turned. E.V. was fumbling with something, but I grabbed
her and jumped.

Electric current, burning, contracting my entire body. I
spasmed away from E.V. The bright blue sky dimmed and
flared. My hands scrabbled across gravel and sand but I
couldn't make them do anything.

E.V. screamed, "No! *No! NOOOOOOOOO!*"

I blinked hard trying to get my sight to behave. We were
alone, in the Empty Quarter. I thought she'd been attacked—
was being attacked. She was on her knees, on the ground,
hunched over, holding herself up with extended arms. Her
pocketbook had spilled open showing a cell phone and money
and a small-unlabeled prescription-medicine bottle. There
was a black cylinder, perhaps seven inches long, clutched in
her other hand.

"I'm okay," I said. I wasn't that sure, but she was horribly
upset. I wanted to reassure her.

"Take me back! Now!"

She was suddenly leaning over me, one hand grabbing
my sweater, the other shaking the black cylinder in my
face.

"What?" My muscles were starting to work again and I
tried to sit up but she shoved me back down again. She was
crying and she looked desperately afraid.

"TAKE ME BACK!"

She jammed the cylinder into my side and the current and the burning came again. My back arched so much my heels and head were the only thing touching the ground. This time I passed out completely.

The sun was dropping below the horizon when I came to. E.V. was coming down the ridge, stumbling, tripping over rocks. She was crying, her eyes so filled with tears she could obviously hardly see.

I sat up. My muscles felt like I'd run a marathon, lactic acid soreness, and there was a burn on my side and another on my back, but I felt like I could jump if I had to.

She had the cell phone in one hand. I didn't see the black rod.

"I didn't know you had a cell phone," I said. I felt insane. *Surely this is what a psychotic break is like?*

She stopped, then threw the phone onto the sand between us. "It's not mine. It belongs to *them*."

Oh, fuck.

She pulled the black rod out of her back pocket and I tensed, but she threw that down, as well. "And that. And those pills." She gestured to where her purse still lay. "I dropped the drink. Why'd I drop the drink? It would be over if I hadn't dropped the drink!"

I looked back at the purse, at the pill bottle. "What kind of pill was it?"

She looked away. "They said it would knock you out. So

they could catch you." She looked back at me and winced. "Yeah, I know. If you'd jumped it wouldn't do any good, even if you passed out after. It had to be poison."

"You knew that?" It felt like my face was going to break. "You knew that and . . . maybe that's why you dropped it." Then the rest of it hit me. "They have your parents." I didn't ask it—I said it.

She dropped to her knees. "They *killed* my father. They cut his fucking throat right in front of me! And then they put the knife against my mother's neck!"

"Oh, God. I'm so sorry." I got up and walked over to her but she shoved me away. She kicked at me and clawed and I stepped back, then dropped down and sat on my heels. "How did they find you? Was it me? Did they track some of my jumps in Trenton?"

She was lying on her side, curled in. "He did it! God-damn him. *He* did it. He wanted to check up on you. After he found that sketch, he got a friend to run a criminal check. They showed up with police badges and he answered *all* their questions. He gave you to them on a silver platter and then they cut his *throat*. Daddy, you *idiot*! The fucking phone won't get a signal! Oh, God. They'll kill them both!"

Oh. "They have your brother, too."

She screamed again and pounded the ground with her fists.

I understood, then. "You went up on the ridge to try and get a signal. If you'd reached them, what would you have done? Come down and finished me? Wait until they came and confirmed my death?"

She jumped up and ran down the arroyo, north. She was still sobbing. I pocketed the phone and, cautiously, the black cylinder, then took up her purse. I let her get about fifty yards away and tripped her, appearing beside her path with my foot outstretched. While she was still down, I hooked the waistline of her jeans and jumped her back to the Hole.

She looked at the bed and collapsed on the floor, sobbing, sobbing.

I couldn't stand it and I jumped away, to the Greenwood Shell petrol station across from her high school. There, in the light of the fluorescents, I looked at the rod. It had four projecting electrodes, sharp, for sticking through clothing, and a slide switch, like on an electric torch. I turned it on, but it didn't spark, so I suspected it was actuated when a partial conductor bridged the points.

I took out the cell phone and called, using the only number in the cell phone's call log.

"Speak." It was Kemp's voice.

"She's dead. I blame you."

I hung up.

I didn't want to hear his threats against Mrs. Kelson or E.V.'s brother, Patrick. I wanted to lower the bar, remove any reason for the bastards to kill them. The phone buzzed in my hand, vibrating, and I thought about throwing it away. Instead I held down the power button until it turned completely off.

I jumped back to the Hole. "Where did they have them?"

She flinched at my voice and looked up at me. "What?"

"Where did they have your mother and brother?"

"They said they'd be moving them. Not to bother with a rescue since they wouldn't be there."

I looked at the ceiling and squeezed my eyes shut. "That's what they *said*. Where were they when they killed your— when they threatened your mother?"

"In the basement. They were all in the basement."

"How many of them were there? That you saw?"

"I don't know. None of the men at the club were the men at the house. There were four at the house."

I jumped.

The house was dark. I'd walked from the petrol station, expecting them to show up in cars or on foot. Hell—I half expected them to parachute in.

But they hadn't.

I remembered the bomb at Alejandra's and I wondered if that's what they had in mind. I jumped away, to the Empty Quarter, and then back again.

Nothing.

I kicked the front door in and jumped away, to the sidewalk.

The dog began barking from the backyard.

I went around the side. There were covered stairs—storm-cellar type, just short of the fence. Booger danced on the other side, barking and wagging his tail at the same time. I tugged at the handle and it opened but I jumped back to the sidewalk before it swung to the side.

Nothing.

I remembered the bomb in San Diego, the one they'd set for movement in the house, unless a door was opened first. They'd used a cell phone trigger in Mexico. How about here? Surely they knew I was here. Even if they were all over at the Teen Club, they could surely feel my jumps.

Or they were waiting inside.

Standing just inside the front door, I flipped the light switch up and jumped back to the sidewalk. The light came on. Nothing exploded. No one jumped out of the coat closet with a knife or a stun gun. I jumped into the house, to the end of the hallway where it ended at the kitchen, then away.

Nothing.

I returned and flipped on the light switch in the kitchen and jumped away.

Outside, I moved down the cellar steps. The door was locked but it had a diamond square glass inset. I showed my head and jumped away.

Nothing.

There was nothing to see—the lights were out and it was pitch black within. I found the inside cellar stairs leading down from the kitchen. There was a light switch at the top. I flipped it and jumped away.

A few minutes later I looked back in the glass inset from the outside cellar door.

Mr. Kelson was on the floor, facedown, his hands cable-tied

behind his back. They'd done it next to the floor drain so there wasn't as much blood as I'd seen in Consuelo's kitchen. On the far wall, pushed up against a leaning pile of disassembled cardboard cartons, Mrs. Kelson and Patrick Kelson were in wooden chairs, their legs duct-taped to the chair's front legs, their arms duct-taped to the chair arms. Duct tape covered their mouths, running all the way around their heads, and there was duct tape across their eyes, too.

I couldn't tell if they were alive or dead.

I couldn't see anyone else through the door but that didn't mean they weren't there.

I jumped into the middle of the room and away, as quickly as I could, so sure I'd trip a motion sensor that I panicked, and arrived back in the Empty Quarter with shreds of cardboard flying around me.

Boy, haven't done that *in a while.*

I jumped back to the sidewalk, outside. The house was still there. Men with knives weren't popping out of the bushes or falling from the sky.

Back in the cellar I could see their labored breath. They'd both soiled themselves and for some reason that made me madder than anything. *They taped them up and just left them.* I wondered how long they'd been without water.

I went to Mrs. Kelson and reached for the tape across her eyes and then froze.

My sloppy jump had dislodged the cardboard stack behind them.

And that's where the bomb was.

It was a military thing, olive drab nylon bag, one end opened, exposing olive drab metal with screw-down terminals and two different multiconductor wires, each leading across the floor to a chair. The wires went up the chair legs under the duct tape and transitioned to the chair seat, tucked under the backs of their knees.

Pressure switch? When you freed them and lifted their bodies off the chairs, did it complete the circuit or break it?

And could the bastards still detonate it remotely?

Call the bomb squad!

Right. And do they detonate it then, when they see all the trucks pull up?

Fuck it!

I gabbed the back of each chair and jumped.

My arms hurt and I couldn't keep Patrick's chair from falling over, but I did slow his fall and we were there, in the Empty Quarter.

Alive.

The wires had broken at the terminals—there was a bit of stripped copper still showing. I wondered if the bomb had gone off or not. Maybe there'd been a delay set.

I took the tape off of their mouths first, and their breathing eased. The tape over their eyes was tricky—I felt like I'd damage their eyelids, so I left it.

Mrs. Kelson groaned.

Patrick stirred. "Who is it? What's happening?"

I thought about reassuring him, then shook my head.

I left them taped to the chairs and jumped them, one at a time, to the sidewalk outside St. Francis Medical Center in Trenton—it was right across from the east side of E.V.'s high school. Someone shouted and I heard footsteps but I didn't even turn around before jumping back to Euclid Avenue in Trenton.

The house hadn't exploded.

I heard the dog barking still, from the backyard, and I was glad.

"Nine-one-one operator. What is the nature of your emergency?"

"There's a dead man and an unexploded bomb in the basement of a house on Euclid Avenue." I gave the street address.

I'd used the cell phone to make the call and when I hung up on the 911 operator's questions, it buzzed again, and I wondered if the operator was calling back.

It was Kemp.

"We'll kill her mother and brother, you know."

Did he expect me to turn myself over to them? Or did they have some way of tracking the phone?

"By all means, kill them," I said. "They deserve it."

I went back to the cellar, quickly, before the bomb squad got there. I wiped the phone off and set it beside Mr. Kelson's body. I was about to jump away again, when I saw a baseball bat leaning in the corner. It wasn't full size—probably left over from Little League. I wondered if it had been Patrick's or E.V.'s.

I looked down at the body.

"Mind if I borrow this?"

The first sirens sounded in the distance and I jumped away.

THIRTEEN

Ends and Beginnings

E.V. was at the table with one of her diet sodas and the bottle of pills. I dropped the bat and jumped across the room, snatching the bottle off the table.

She flinched. In a flat voice she said, "I wasn't going to. I thought about it—I really did."

I threw the pill canister across the cave and into the old entrance shaft.

"Why?" I asked. "The bastards are already doing enough. You want to do their work for them?"

She just looked down at the table. She wouldn't look up.

Love me. Take me back to bed and love me. Make it like it never happened.

"I'm sorry," I said. "I'm sorry about your fath—"

"Goddamn it! Couldn't you have lied? *Why'd you have to tell me your real name? Why couldn't you have lied! You lied about the other stuff!*"

I'd already had the same thought. Her father would probably still be alive if I'd made up a name. Hell, I could've been Paully MacLand, the bastard. I took her elbow, to pull her up, and she lashed out at me. I blocked it automatically. Years of karate were good for something, it turned out. Keep your girlfriend from beating on you.

Something wrong there.

I shoved her back down into the chair and while she struggled to get her balance back, trying to keep the chair from tipping over backward, I stepped in and jumped her to the sidewalk across from her high school.

She twisted away, hunching in on herself, then looked around. "What—why here?" She was staring west, toward the high school.

I gestured behind her toward the medical center, at the large internally lit red cross with the words EMERGENCY ROOM

265

beside it. "Your brother and mother are in there. They're okay—probably dehydrated, but physically okay." I shrugged.

Anger, rage, fear, terror, grief—she'd finally managed to hide those, to push them to the background—but this, hope, was too much. I had to walk her the rest of the way, supporting her through the waiting room door, to the first row of seats.

It wasn't crowded. A woman in scrubs came forward, concern furrowing her face. E.V.'s grief was extravagant, unmitigated, loud.

I saw her safely seated and turned to the nurse. "Her mother and brother were just dropped off here. Uh, there was duct tape involved."

The nurse's eyes widened. "The police are—"

I held up my hand and something in my face made her recoil and stop talking, midsentence.

I put E.V.'s pocketbook in her lap, touched her hair and said, "I hope you never have to lie about who you are, E.V." I took a deep shuddering breath and felt the tears coming.

I no longer cared who saw me or not.

"Good-bye."

I jumped.

I could still smell E.V. on the bedding. Hell, her coat was still lying there, with mine, on top of the dresser. I took it with me to the bed and buried my face in it.

It was all mixed up—stuff from Mum and Dad, stuff from Sam and Consuelo, Henry. E.V. E.V.'s grief for her father, a man who'd really just wanted to make sure his daughter was safe. I wish he'd left well enough alone. Everyone would've been happier or, at least, alive. I wanted to be angry with him but hard as I tried, it all turned inward.

After all, what was the common denominator, if not me?

It was the worst night, the longest night.

I'd jumped that day, accidentally, when Paully charged me. Mum and Dad were dead.

Going to live with Alejandra had doomed Sam and Consuelo. If I hadn't sent the INS in, would the agents still be alive?

If I hadn't used my real name with E.V. or real details about where I lived. Me, me, me, it was all me.

I hated myself. I even thought about the pills down the tunnel. I fell asleep and had nightmares. I woke up and the reality was just as bad.

E.V.'s smell was a torment and a comfort and I thought about wrapping myself in her coat, going down the old tunnel, and getting the pills.

I soaked in that for a while—wallowed, really—but then the other common denominator gradually surfaced.

Them.

I snatched San Diego Sheriff's Department investigator Bob Vigil from the parking lot at the Lemon Grove substation. He'd just shut the door on his car and was turning toward the building when I appeared, grabbed his collar, and jumped.

He came down on his back, hard, in the Empty Quarter,

but his hand came out from under his coat with his service automatic pretty darn fast.

I wasn't there anymore.

I watched him for a few minutes, sitting in the shade on top of the ridge. He tried his cell phone but it didn't get a signal. He put away his gun after a few minutes and I jumped, jabbing him in the right arm with the black cylinder. He fell over in a very satisfying way and I had his gun, his Mace, his extra clips, his cell phone, his wallet, and his handcuffs before he was able to sit up, much less stand.

When I'd first grabbed him, in the parking lot, I'd felt the stiff edge of his Kevlar vest. I'd been planning to shock him in the back, but I changed to the arm instead.

I didn't bother threatening him with the gun. In fact, I popped the clip out and then aimed it off to the side, to see if there was a bullet chambered.

There was. We both flinched at the noise.

"How's that shoulder, Bob?"

He glared at me. I pulled up my shirt, on the left side, and twisted to show him my scar. "See that, Bob? That's where your friends tried for my kidney. Pretty, huh?"

His expression went from angry to wary.

"I'm not happy about that, Bob. I think that's pretty understandable." I jumped twenty feet directly behind him and said, "Do you *understand,* Bob?"

He twisted so fast he tangled his feet and staggered off to one side. "What *are* you?" he asked hoarsely.

"Didn't they tell you, Bob? Didn't they give you some justification?" I jumped again, twenty feet off to his left, and he recoiled again. "You set me up. What did you think would happen?"

"They said you were a threat to, uh, national security."

"A sixteen-year-old kid? A threat to national security?" I opened his wallet. He had three twenties and a few credit cards but there was a zippered compartment behind the cash. I pulled the zipper, spread it wide, and whistled. I held it out to display a thick sheaf of hundred dollar bills. "How good *is* the pay at the sheriff's department?"

"Go fuck yourself," he said. "I don't have to tell you anything!"

"Oh," I said quietly to myself, "I really think you *do*." This time I jabbed him in the right buttock with the shock stick. He dropped to the side and yelled.

I crouched down about five feet away. "I'm not the police. I'm not *constrained* by your rules of evidence and prisoner treatment." He was watching me and twitching. I swayed to one side and his eyes followed me. "Of course, *you* don't seem that constrained by the rules, either. I almost believed you about the national security thing."

He snarled.

"I don't even care about you. I don't know if they told you they'd be trying to knife me or not. But I want to know what they told you. How they contacted you. If—no—*how* they wanted you to contact them if I showed up again."

I played with the black cylinder, passing it from hand to hand. "Why don't you just tell me? You do, and it checks out, I'll let you go."

He swore at me in Spanish so I switched to that.

"*Este es tu momento de la verdad, Roberto.* Literally. Your moment of truth. They didn't quite get me, but they killed someone else two days ago and I'm not happy about that. You can probably tell. Not only can I do this—"

I feinted toward his leg with the cylinder and he cried out, "Stop!"

I rocked back on my heels. "But I can also give information to the FBI about your involvement in that murder. They cut his throat while his hands were tied behind his back. And then there's the INS—they'd probably like to know that you've been taking bribes from the people who killed six of theirs."

I sort of smiled but I could feel the wrongness of it, like fingers tugging my features around. "I'm not sure you'd see trial."

Now *this,* where the physical stuff didn't seem to be getting through, actually seemed to work.

"It's on my phone. In my contacts. There's a number labeled *saltador*! But that's all I know, I swear!"

I laughed out loud. *Saltador* is Spanish for vaulter or jumper.

I left him there while I checked for a signal. I got one at the Texaco petrol station out on Old 80, barely. I jumped to the ridgetop where I used to meet Sam and Consuelo and found that it was closer to the cell tower, three bars on the signal-strength indicator.

Vigil was standing when I got back but looking around, confused. The sun was high overhead and he wasn't sure which direction was which. I threw his wallet to him, high, and as he jumped up into the air to grab it, I jumped him and spilled him onto the ridgetop.

"Hey!" he yelled. "I told you what you wanted to know!"

I said soothingly, "Yes, you did. But did you want me to shock you again, to get you here? That was the alternative."

I took the shock stick out of my pocket again. "Now. All I want you to do is tell them that you convinced me they were following you, that you're on *my* side, and I've agreed to another meeting out at Sam Coulton's place. Uh, nobody's moved in there, have they?"

"Hell no. Eight people died there. The cousin who ended up with it wants to sell but nobody is interested."

"Okay. Tell them it's set for three o'clock."

He looked at his watch. "That'll only give them an hour to get out there."

"So it will." I flipped open his phone and found the entry and dialed it.

He did it as I'd told him and, after he told them when and where, he said, "So, I'll see you—" He tilted the phone in his hand and stared at it. "They hung up."

I held my hand out for the phone.

His fingers closed around it and I lifted the shock tube.

"Hey, it's my phone."

"Sure," I said.

He relaxed and I jumped, only two feet to the side, and kicked the phone out of his hand. It really flew, high, higher, and came down in the brush thirty feet away.

He was clutching his hand to his chest and swearing. I walked over, picked up a fist-sized rock, and hit the phone three times.

I set his gun and ammunition and the Mace and handcuffs on the fragments of plastic and circuit board. "See the highway?" I said pointing at the distant gray line.

He held up his good hand and flipped me the bird.

"I bet you can walk it in about two hours."

I jumped away.

I was on my back, under Sam's couch, my nose just clearing the cotton batten and steel leaf springs. If I'd been one inch thicker, it wouldn't have worked.

I heard their footsteps first, but just barely. Didn't hear a car so I presumed they'd parked their vehicle somewhere off the road, out of earshot. They came sooner that I expected, but I'd been there for thirty minutes and was reasonably confident that they hadn't felt me arrive.

Not unless they'd been camping within range.

The door was locked but they opened it. Didn't know if they had a key or if they'd picked it but they didn't force it— that would've given the game away.

They checked the house carefully, though, opening closets

and cabinets, peeking up into the attic crawlspace. I'd been planning on waiting up there, myself, but it was like an oven so I'd checked the couch on a whim.

Fortunately, they didn't.

"What about the grounds? He could be out there."

Young voice, American English, nervous, it seemed.

"Relax," said the other, older, more confident. There was something faintly European in his accent. A trace of Scandinavian—like a young Max von Sydow. "If he's already here he'll still have to show himself when Vigil arrives."

"Kemp should be here."

"We kill jumpers. We're not jumpers ourselves! How's he supposed to get here from New Jersey in time?"

"I'd just feel better. He's had more experience, right? With grown jumpers? All I've ever dealt with are the kids."

"Well, yes—only Roland's group has more experience."

"Christ. *Roland.* Now that's one scary paladin."

The older man breathed out sharply, an exasperated sound. "Go watch out the back but be careful. Don't show yourself. Don't scare him off. He could approach on foot, but don't forget he knows this house. He could jump in. This one . . . if we get him, well, it will reflect well on us. Roland has been reading the reports and he's not pleased."

I barely heard the footsteps as the other man moved off.

I'd give them that—they were stealthy bastards.

Only two of them. Only two of them in the area, then. They'd have sent more if there'd been more. I just had that feeling.

273

All I've ever dealt with are the kids. Huh. I remembered the man in the car, back in Lechlade, when I was five. I remembered *the* night when I was nine. Go after 'em when they're young enough and they're *easy*.

All right, fuckers, time to pick on someone your own *size*.

By rolling my head to the side I could see under the skirting at the base of the couch. Across the carpet I could just see partway up his boots, brown, soft soled, back near the hallway, where he could look out both the front windows and also step back out of sight when someone showed up.

I didn't change posture as I jumped, staying down on the floor, jabbing the shock stick up into the back of his thigh. He got off a shot but was unable to aim, and the cables and spikes smashed one of the front windows as he fell over. For good measure I jabbed him again in the side, then, hearing footsteps, I jumped away, to the old stable across the graveled front yard.

He didn't use the door—he jumped out through the smashed window, then rolled sideways across the porch to his feet. He charged across the yard like a winger heading out of the scrum for the goal, changing directions randomly to avoid the opposing players. He had one of those guns, the spike and cable projectors, a hand on the handle and the other cradling the barrel.

I timed him, though, and on his next change of direction, I jumped, jabbing with the shock stick.

His foot caught me in the stomach and I was still rising in the air when I jumped away.

274

JUMPER: GRIFFIN'S STORY

I came down in the Empty Quarter, stunned, unable to move. I was trying to inhale but it wasn't working. I jabbed at my diaphragm with my fingers and then it caught, like a motor, and my first breath turned into a raging, hacking cough.

Damn, he's fast.

He reminded me of the brown belt who'd taken first at Birmingham. I looked around for the shock stick but it was gone, probably lying on the ground back at Sam's place.

I jumped to the Hole, still coughing, intending to get the spike gun, the one I'd taken from Mateo in La Crucecita, but I saw the baseball bat instead.

Right.

I jumped back to the living room. The first man was still down, but he was fumbling with the gun—he'd opened the breech and was pulling out the spent cartridge. An unfired one lay on his stomach, ready to be inserted.

I took one sideways step and smashed the gun away with the bat, swinging up, underhanded. The gun smashed against the far wall but he never stopped moving and suddenly there was a knife in his hand, like it'd sprouted there.

I brought the bat back down on the return swing, smashing into his extended hand. The knife stuck in the floor, quivering, and he yelled.

The yell did it. I'd heard that yell before.

He'd been there, *that* night.

I'd shot him with the paintball gun in the bollocks twice and I'd hit him multiple times in the face with the barrel of the gun. I could see faint scars.

I backhanded him in the face with the bat.

Junior was at the door, the gun rising. I remembered what Dad had told me so long ago: *Don't let anyone even* point *a weapon at you.*

I jumped to the porch, behind him, but this time I was expecting the foot that lashed out toward me and I twisted aside as I brought the bat down on the back of his extended knee.

I heard something pop in the joint and he screamed, but he still tried to turn, to bring the gun to bear through the doorway, but the bat got there first, smashing the barrel up and back and . . . it went off.

Both spikes came up through his jaw, one ripping through the carotid artery on his left side, spraying blood as he fell back. His legs spasmed once, twice, and he lay still.

I felt my stomach heave and I knew I was going to be sick, but then, halfway off the porch, hunched over, I stopped myself. I straightened up and took two deep breaths through my nose, then turned around and made myself look.

He bled quite a lot. Sam's heir, the distant cousin, had put new carpet in. He wasn't going to be happy.

I jumped past the body and the spreading stain.

The older man, the one who'd been there *that* night, wasn't breathing. A trickle of blood ran out of one ear. His eyes were wide and staring and one pupil was noticeably larger than the other.

"Good."

I said it aloud and it echoed in the room, louder than I expected, and harsher.

I swam at the beach in Oaxaca, Bahía Chacacual, fighting higher surf than usual. There must've been a storm farther south, down Guatemala way, to send these swells north. I found myself rubbing my face under the water and realized I was still trying to get the blood off.

If it's not off now, it's not coming off. Get over it.

I body-surfed back to shore and jumped up into the jungle where my showers were. It was all too easy to remember E.V. standing here, slippery, warm, and naked, and I cut the shower short.

Her coat still lay at the foot of the bed.

I jumped into New York City at rush hour and rode the train down to Trenton, walking through the streets with all the commuters. Mr. Kelson's body was lying in state at the Gruerio Funeral Home until the services on Saturday. My plan was to leave the coat and let her discover it but when the attendant ushered me into the chapel, she was sitting there.

The attendant stepped back outside and I went up to the front row and sat on the far end of the bench. The casket was open but I had no desire to view the departed.

"I brought your coat."

She was looking at me, her eyes wide, the corners of her mouth hooked down.

"Won't they come back? Won't they know you're here?"

I shrugged. "I took the train. I'll leave on the train. I won't jump from anywhere near here. Unless I *have* to."

She turned away and covered her face with both hands. I kept expecting her to say something, but she didn't.

"You could've trusted me," I finally said. "The result would've been almost exactly the same. Only we—"

She didn't respond. After a moment I got up and walked to the door.

That's when she said, "I'm glad you brought the coat. It was *his*." She jerked her head toward the casket. "He never gave it to me but I started wearing it when it no longer dragged on the floor. And he never said a word."

I took a wandering route back to the station, looping east, far from her house, and took the train to Philadelphia.

When it clanked passed Croydon, I jumped away to the Hole.

On the train, people all around, I'd pushed forward, numb.

Now I couldn't even move. I stood hunched over, between the table and the bed, my mouth half open. I was standing with my back to the plywood gallery.

Oh.

I made myself turn, walk forward, and sit on the edge of the bed.

The light was already on so E.V.'s face, as I'd sketched it in Regent's Park, was there, relaxed, innocent—unmarred, unmarked by tragedy, by horror. The shape of her collarbone, the dip of the sweater's neckline, the tracery of lace at the edge of her bra, the outline of her breasts.

278

And her eyes.

Those eyes would never look at me like that again.

I tore it into pieces and then I tore those pieces and then I tore those pieces. I ended up with a pile of coin-sized scraps on the table, flecks of art stock. My traitor hands started sorting them, looking for fragments that matched, like a jigsaw puzzle.

In the Empty Quarter I made a fire of dead mesquite out in the middle of the wash, adding more and more wood until it was like a pyre.

When the flames were taller than me, I threw the fragments of the sketch into the fire and watched them vanish almost immediately—flame, ash, and then sparks drifting into the sky.

Triangulation.

Honesty is the best policy, that's what they say, but it was a disaster for me. I should never have mentioned Borrego Springs. But I had plenty of warning. They drove around *listening*. Waiting for me to jump so they could figure out where my lair was.

The sheep farmers had started throwing coyotes down my shaft again and I was getting ready to make another visit, though this time I was considering taking the baseball bat.

I'd jumped to a ridge near Fish Creek campground with my binoculars, trying to catch the Keyhoe brothers on their ATVs, when a truck kicking up a dust trail in the wash below suddenly swerved and braked.

I stepped behind a boulder and took a look with the binoculars.

Three men. Kemp and the big man from Oaxaca and someone I didn't know. They'd felt the jump. They were looking up the ridge.

I walked away, down the other side of the ridge toward the gypsum mine. I was considering just walking away until I was at least eight miles out of range, but I didn't know what direction they'd drive their truck.

And anyway, if they were *this* close, they'd already felt me jump from the Hole multiple times. They were probably taking bearings, triangulating.

I jumped away, to the park headquarters, then to the Keyhoe ranch, where I smashed a window and riled up the dogs, then jumped away to New York and had a hot dog in Battery Park.

After thirty minutes I sighed heavily.

Time to move.

On the outskirts of Rennes I found a farmer with a shed to rent. It was dry with a good roof and a stone floor well off the damp ground and he took a year's rent in cash without asking for an ID of any kind.

"Drouges?"

"Bien sûr que non!"

Drugs indeed!

I jumped back to the Hole and transferred the wall of sketches, my dresser, and the weapons I'd taken from them so far. I looked at everything else—the batteries, the generator, the lights, the bed, and the furniture and decided against it. I hesitated over the shelf of self-study materials, then I shook my head.

I jumped to San Diego and stole six barbecue canisters of propane gas from a gas distributor and brought them back.

Then I spent three hours doing nothing but jumping from one end of the Hole to the other end.

If the bastards didn't feel that, then what good were they?

Every hour I jumped to the surface, right above the Hole. It wouldn't feel much different to them compared to underground, unless they were already there, but they weren't.

But I heard them coming.

I walked away, back into the boulders, and made my way up the hill. I had my binoculars and the baseball bat, and I was ready to play.

There were six of them in two different all-wheel-drive trucks and when they left the vehicles they fanned out in two groups of three. They looked inward, toward each other, and I realized it was a way to watch each other's back, because if your enemy could materialize in your midst, you had to look *everywhere*.

I waited until the two groups were well apart and took out one of Kemp's group, smashing his knee, taking advantage of his fast reflexes and hitting him as he lashed out.

Both Kemp and his other teammate fired their spikes toward me, but they missed because I'd jumped away, and they missed their teammate because he'd fallen on his ass.

I snagged Kemp by the collar while he was reloading, and

dropped him in the Hole. When he twisted and fired at me, I jumped to the other end of the cave where I'd left my own equipment.

My spikes and cable caught him across his chest and pinned him to the plywood wall. It was ironic. That was the sheet that still said "Sensitives" on it, though the sketches were in France now.

He was struggling out from under the cable and I wondered if the charge was gone. Or if he was just tough. I fired another, lower, across his thighs, and saw him spasm. I put another across his chest and arms, and then another, shoulder high.

He carried his knife in a sleeve sheath, a mechanical thing that popped it into his hand. He had a shock stick in his back pocket and six cartridges for his gun in the loops of his belt. I took his cell phone and his wallet, too, and put them on the table.

There were three different IDs. None of them for Kemp. I guess I'd made it too hot for him under that name. I took a jump back to the surface, and then to the metal ladder leading down into the mine. It stank—the dead coyotes were still there—but I didn't mind somehow.

I returned to Kemp and jabbed him with the shock stick.

Oh, good. I'd been thinking he had some sort of immunity. The plywood, thick, three-quarter-inch stuff, flexed like cardboard.

While he spasmed, I got a chair and straddled it, arms resting across the back.

His twitching lessened and I said, "Paladin. Hmph. That's an odd name for someone who goes around killing children."

I had his full attention suddenly. He hadn't been looking particularly good but when I said that he went pasty white.

"Am I not supposed to know that?" I asked innocently. "Which part am I not supposed to know? That you guys are paladins? Or that you spend most of your time offing little kids?"

He was staring at me like he'd made a mistake, like he'd thought I was one thing, and he'd discovered I was another. "Listen, boy—"

I jabbed him in the stomach with the shock stick, jumping forward past the chair.

As he went into another set of convulsions, I walked back around to the chair. "We got off on the wrong foot, I think. Probably when you *killed my parents.* Maybe you thought I didn't *like* my parents but I gotta tell you, you were wrong about that. Then there was Sam and Consuelo . . . now I'm confused. Why *did* you kill them? Wouldn't it have been better to leave them alive, to see if I'd make contact again? Would *Roland* have done it that way?"

He began thrashing again, but it wasn't the shock stick. He was trying to get out of the cables. Was it the mention of Roland's name? This time I kicked him in the bollocks.

"Christ, would you settle down!" I shouted. He was having trouble breathing and he was making little groaning sounds. I pointed at his groin. "Oh, yeah. And then you had to go and mess with my love life! That was really the last straw."

I looked back over at my books, the schoolwork, the novels I loved.

"I used to be a nice kid. Probably the kind of kid you're used to, the kind of kid who dies nice and quiet when you show up with your knives and spiky guns and cables and shock sticks and all."

I jumped away, back to the other side of the cave, where it led out to the vertical shaft. They'd broken open the grating and I could hear them coming down the ladder.

I returned to Kemp and began stacking the propane tanks on top of the table, two rows of three. When I was done, I went down to the other end of the room, to my little twelve-volt refrigerator, and took out a pack of dinner candles.

I'd bought them with E.V. in mind, for a romantic dinner.

I lit two of the candles, dripped wax atop the fridge, and anchored them there, burning brightly.

Romantic.

"So, do you have a secret headquarters, Kemp? I mean, someplace where you guys hang out, shoot darts, heft a few pints, eat paladin cakes, and practice killing little kids?"

He licked his lips. "Alejandra," he said.

I kicked him again. Same place. "Don't even *say* her name!"

He was reaching. I hoped he was reaching, but no matter what, I wasn't going to play their games anymore.

"Why do you guys do it? Why are you after me? Why do you go around killing us?"

He looked at me and I saw hate and I saw fear, but he didn't speak and I was sick of hitting on him.

I opened three of the six propane tank valves and jumped away, to the top of the hill above.

I counted to ten. For a moment, I thought the candles had gone out. Then I felt it in my feet, the shock, followed by the rumble, echoing against the hill.

Down below, the mineshaft opening spat dust and smoke and, oddly, a near perfect smoke ring that spread as it rose until it was over a hundred feet in diameter.

Their trucks had cracked windows but the guy I'd injured first was still alive, shaken and staring around.

I thought about taking him away and playing with him, maybe extracting some information about this Roland guy, but I was tired.

Let him explain *this* to the park rangers.

I had a lead on a cell of three paladins who operated around the Gare de Lyon train station and I was drawing them out with a series of jumps, figuring out who were the Sensitives.

I'd identified one working the news kiosk and another, a waiter at Le Train Bleu, but I'd had no luck on the third and didn't want to move until I had.

I was eating *pain au chocolat* and between the flaky crust all down my jacket and the sticky chocolate on my face and fingers, I was making a right mess of things when a group of Spanish tourists went by following their tour guide. She was discussing the history of the station in perfect Castilian, but the voice wrenched my head around and widened my eyes.

She'd dyed her hair blond and cut it short, but it was her, slightly thinner, just as beautiful as ever.

As Alejandra came closer I turned away, pulling napkins from my paper bag and dabbing at the chocolate on my face. I soaked in every word, every bit of the warm, musical voice.

I wanted to run after her, to grab her, to hold her. I wanted her to hold *me*.

I didn't turn around until she was gone.

People surrounded me, moving through the station like schools of fish in a reef, like milling sheep. Meeting each other, talking, kissing, hurrying to make a train, their thoughts on their destinations or points of origin or just dinner.

But not me.

You don't have to drive or walk or even *jump* to get to the Empty Quarter.

Sometimes it comes to you.

The waiter I'd already identified talked briefly to a customer passing out of the restaurant. This man wandered around the train station for five minutes, watching the timetables, then abruptly went to the news kiosk. There he bought a newspaper, and talked briefly to the clerk, my other subject—only a few sentences, but more than were necessary to buy a paper.

Hello, boys.

I jumped.